# Heartland

## After the Storm

*by* Lauren Brooke

SCHOLASTIC INC.

New York  Toronto  London  Auckland  Sydney
Mexico City  New Delhi  Hong Kong

*For Jane, who taught me everything*
*that is true about horses*

ISBN 0-439-13022-0

Heartland series created by Working Partners Ltd, London.

Photo credit for horse on cover:
Ray Woolfe/Photo Researchers, Inc.
The poem "The life that I have" copyright © 1958 by Leo Marks.

Copyright © 2000 by Working Partners Ltd.
Published by Scholastic Inc. All rights reserved.

12 11 10 9 8 7 6 5 4 3                                    0 1 2 3 4 5/0
Printed in the U.S.A.                                                40
First Scholastic printing, June 2000

# Chapter One

Amy tried to scream as she saw her mom open the driver's door to the pickup. But no words would come out. She wanted to stop her, but she couldn't move. She could only watch, horrified, as her mother put the key in the ignition and started the engine.

And then the dream sped forward.

Now they were both in the pickup. Rain pounded against the windshield, blurring Amy's vision. And the trailer behind them was shaking violently as the bay stallion kicked out in fear. Amy tried hard to wake herself up, but the dream tightened its hold on her. She was trapped in the same nightmare she had been having over and over again for the past month.

Her mother's hands gripped the steering wheel tightly.

"This is insane," she muttered, her blue eyes looking into Amy's. "We should never have come out in this."

"Stop!" Amy sobbed desperately. "Stop, Mom, please stop." But Marion didn't hear her.

A flash of lightning split the dark sky, and the clattering of hooves in the trailer was drowned out by a huge crash of thunder overhead.

Amy started to scream when she saw the tall, swaying trees that loomed on the road ahead. Branches closed over the top of the pickup, banging and scraping along the roof of the trailer. A long, drawn-out creak of breaking wood was followed by a clap of thunder so loud that it sounded like a cannon had been fired. Straight in front of them, a tree started to fall slowly into the road.

*"No!"* Amy screamed. "Please, no!"

"Amy! Amy! Wake up!"

Amy suddenly felt her shoulder being shaken. She opened her eyes. She was lying on a hard wooden floor. Her grandfather was bending over her, his forehead creased in concern.

"Grandpa," Amy said, sitting up in confusion.

She breathed in a faint, familiar smell of perfume. Photographs of horses stared down at her from the walls. She was in her mother's room. A coat was slung over a chair just where her mom had left it the day of the accident. The hairbrush on the dressing table was coated in a fine layer of dust, a few blond hairs caught in the bristles. Nothing in the room had changed for six weeks, not since the night of the storm when Marion Fleming had died.

At the sight of all the familiar things Amy felt her stomach twist. "What am I doing here?"

Jack Bartlett must have seen the shock on her face. "It's OK, honey," he said reassuringly. "You were sleepwalking."

"It was that dream again," Amy stammered, getting to her feet. The air in the room felt still and quiet. Sweat prickled through her long hair as she looked around.

"Come on, it's over now," her grandpa said soothingly. "Let's get you back to your own room." He put his arm around her shoulders.

Just then her mom's bedroom door opened. Lou, Amy's older sister, stood in the doorway. "Are you all right?" she asked, her short blond hair tousled from sleep. "I heard screaming."

"It's OK," Jack said quickly as he steered Amy toward the door. "Amy had a nightmare and was sleepwalking."

"Oh, Amy," Lou said, moving swiftly to Amy's side.

"I'm OK," Amy said, pulling away from Grandpa and pushing past Lou to the door. She just wanted to get out of the room. She could hardly breathe. It was too much to bear — knowing that Mom was never coming back.

The sheets on her bed felt cool. She pulled them over her. Grandpa and Lou came to the doorway. Out of the corner of her eye she could see Grandpa say something to Lou in a low voice.

Lou nodded. "Sleep well, Amy. See you in the morning," she said softly, and left.

Grandpa came over and sat on the edge of Amy's bed.

"I'm OK, Grandpa," Amy told him. "You should go to bed now, too."

"I can stay for a bit," Grandpa said.

Amy felt too exhausted to argue. She lay back against the pillows. As her eyes began to shut, the nightmare flickered around the edges of her consciousness. She shuddered and blinked.

"Oh, Grandpa," she said, opening her eyes quickly.

"Don't worry, I'm here," Grandpa said gently. He stroked her hair. "Go to sleep now, honey."

When Amy awoke in the morning, Grandpa had left. As always, the first thought that flashed into her mind was the hot, quick hope that the last six weeks had never happened. But as she saw the pale morning light filtering through her curtains, reality hit her with an icy certainty — her mom was dead, and it was her fault.

Amy sat up, wrapping her arms around her knees. If she hadn't been so desperate to rescue Spartan, the bay stallion, from the barn where he'd been abandoned by thieves, then Mom would never have gone out in that storm, and the accident would never have happened. Amy was the one who had pleaded with her mom to go. She wanted to save Spartan, but in the end she had lost so much more. A sickening feeling of guilt gripped her heart.

Getting out of bed, Amy pulled on a pair of jeans and went to open the curtains. From her window she could see Heartland's front stable block and the patchwork of paddocks filled with horses grazing and dozing in the quiet of the early morning sun. Stepping over the clutter of clothes and magazines on her floor, Amy hurried downstairs. She decided to go ahead and start on the barn chores. She didn't want to think about Mom — just as she didn't want to think about what the day ahead held for her.

Later that afternoon, Amy stood in one of the stalls in the stable block and shook a flake of straw onto a thick, fresh bed. Dust particles floated and danced in the shafts of warm sunlight that shone in over the half door. She thought about Spartan. Tomorrow he would be standing exactly where she was now. For a moment she almost wanted to be sick. Life felt so unfair.

"Almost done?" Ty, Heartland's seventeen-year-old stable hand, asked as he looked over the door. He must have noticed the look on Amy's face, because his expression suddenly softened with concern. "Amy? Are you OK?" he asked, walking in.

Amy nodded, not trusting herself to speak.

"Hey," Ty said softly. He looked around the stall. "Are you worried about Spartan?" Amy nodded again. "It'll be fine," he said, squeezing her arm sympathetically. "You'll see."

From down the yard came the sound of the farmhouse door opening. "Amy! Ty!" Grandpa called. "It's almost time to go."

Amy went to the door. "We're coming!"

"I'd better get cleaned up," Ty said. "I'll see you down at the house in a minute." Leaving the stall he hurried toward the tack room.

As Amy shut the half door she glanced around the stall one more time. The very next day Spartan would be there. He would look over this door, waiting to be fed, to be groomed, to be cared for, just like any of the other horses at Heartland. Amy shivered. She couldn't kid herself. Spartan would never be just another horse to her.

She walked slowly toward the white-painted farmhouse and let herself in through the back door. Grandpa and Lou were talking quietly in the kitchen. They were both dressed in dark clothes. On the table lay a big bunch of white lilies tied with a black ribbon. They filled the air with a sweet, heavy scent.

"We have to leave soon," Jack Bartlett said. "We said we'd meet Scott and Matt at five thirty."

Amy nodded. "I have to change out of my barn clothes," she said, heading for the stairs.

Reaching her bedroom, Amy grabbed a brush and ran it quickly through her light brown hair before twisting it up on top of her head with a clip. Leaving her jeans and T-shirt in a heap, she pulled on a long black sleeveless dress. She checked her reflection in the mirror on her desk. Her gray eyes looked large in her pale face.

Her gaze fell on the framed photograph of her mom that she kept by the mirror. She picked it up. It was one of her favorite pictures. Mom, standing by a pasture gate, laughing as she stroked Pegasus. It had been taken just a few weeks before the accident. Amy felt a stab of pain in her chest.

"Amy!" She heard Lou calling up the stairs.

Putting the photograph down, Amy picked up a piece of paper from her desk, folded it quickly, and put it in her pocket.

Lou was standing at the bottom of the staircase, her normally composed face showing signs of tension. "Ready?" she asked in her subtle accent, one of the obvious clues that Lou had attended boarding school and college in England before moving to New York.

Amy fiddled with the piece of paper in her pocket. "Yeah, I'm ready."

They went through to the kitchen.

Ty was by the door. His wavy dark hair was combed back, and he had put on a clean white shirt and black pants. His eyes met Amy's with a look of concern and support. She managed a faint smile in return.

Jack opened the back door. "Well then, let's go."

They drove to the cemetery in silence. Scott Trewin, the local equine vet, and his younger brother, Matt, were waiting in the parking lot when they arrived.

"Hi," Matt said quietly as Amy got out of the car.

Matt and Amy went to the same high school and were good friends. In the past, Matt had suggested that he was interested in them becoming more than just friends, but today his face showed nothing but kind sympathy and concern. He smiled warmly. "How are you doing?"

Amy nodded. "Not so bad."

Walking across the memorial ground, Amy thought about the service. That morning her mother's headstone had been placed to mark her grave, and now Amy had the chance to say a proper good-bye. The official funeral had been held six weeks ago, a few days after the accident, while Amy was still lying unconscious in the hospital.

The group reached the shady corner where Marion's headstone had been placed. There was an older headstone to the left. Although it was weathered by the years, the plot had been carefully tended. Amy watched her grandpa's gaze fall on it. Walking up to it, he gently touched it and closed his eyes.

It was the grave of Jack's wife, Amy's grandmother, who had died even before Lou, who was twenty-three, had been born.

After a moment, Grandpa returned to the small group. He cleared his throat. "Well, thanks for coming. As you all know, we are here today to say a final farewell to Marion." He looked around at everyone. "A daughter, a mother, a friend. Each of us has our own special memories of her. She made us laugh, she dried our tears, she listened, she helped, she loved. She cared passionately for all the horses that she took in and healed at Heartland. Marion's love was boundless, and I am so proud that she was my daughter."

As Grandpa spoke, Amy focused on the light gray headstone, the soil around its base still fresh and slightly damp, flowers heaped on the grave. It felt as though Grandpa's words were washing over her — they weren't registering at all. She stared dry-eyed at the inscription on the stone and read her mom's name, the year she was born, and the year of her death, over and over again. She, Lou, and Grandpa had chosen the inscription together. It read:

*Her spirit will live on at Heartland forever.*

"Amy," Grandpa said softly, breaking through her thoughts. "Will you read the poem you have chosen to remember your mom?"

Amy walked forward, and kneeling, laid the lilies at the base of the headstone. Then she took her place again beside Lou, who squeezed her hand, tears welling in her eyes. Amy took the folded piece of paper from her pocket and opened it up.

"Mom loved this poem," she said quietly. "She had it pinned to the mirror in her bedroom. Daddy gave it to her when her first horse died. It's called 'The life that I have,' and it's by Leo Marks." Looking down at the creased piece of paper she started to read:

"The life that I have
Is all that I have
And the life that I have
Is yours."

As Amy read she noticed that Lou was fighting to stay composed, and her grandpa was brushing a hand across his eyes. Amy waited for her own tears to overwhelm her, but none came. She read on, her voice clear, her mind numb.

"The love that I have
Of the life that I have
Is yours and yours and yours.
A sleep I shall have
A rest I shall have
Yet death will be but a pause.
For the peace of my years,
In the long green grass
Will be yours and yours and yours."

As she folded up the paper, Amy heard a stifled sob come from Lou. Feelings of desperation welled up in her. Why wasn't she feeling anything? Why wasn't she crying? After she returned the poem to her pocket, she walked slowly forward. "Good-bye, Mom," she whispered, touching the headstone. "We'll take good care of Heartland. I promise."

Grandpa walked up behind her and put his hand on her shoulder. She turned, and he kissed her on the forehead. They stood silent for a moment.

As the little group moved slowly back to the parking lot, each one wrapped in his or her own thoughts and memories, Ty walked alongside Amy. "You OK?" he asked, his eyes looking deep into hers.

Amy knew that he must be surprised that she wasn't crying. It just wasn't her nature to keep her feelings to herself. But it wasn't a conscious decision. She felt all sorts of emotions whirling inside of her. She wanted to cry, she really did, but something was stopping her. "I'm fine," she replied. She smiled gratefully. "Thanks for coming, Ty."

"I wanted to come." Ty shook his head, his eyes dark and intense. "Your mom was an amazing person. She really made me believe that I had a special way of understanding horses. I dropped out of high school because I wanted to work with her. I knew that I could learn so much more from her than school would ever teach me. . . ." His voice echoed his confusion and loss. "I just can't believe she's gone."

Amy touched his arm. Quickly, he covered her hand with his own.

"Amy." Amy collected her thoughts and turned. Scott came up to her. "That poem was beautiful," he said, looking down at her. "I can see why it meant so much to Marion."

"I know," Amy said. Scott looked her full in the face and impulsively she changed the subject, hoping he wouldn't notice her lack of tears. "How . . . how's Spartan?" As the name left her lips her stomach tightened. *Spartan.* Scott had chosen the name. Spartan wasn't the easiest thing to think about just then.

"He's very unsettled," Scott replied. "Physically he's on the mend, but mentally he's still traumatized. He's extremely nervous and wary of people. The accident really got to him."

Guilt flooded through Amy.

Scott looked at her reassuringly. "But I think you'll be able to get through to him, Amy," he said. "If anyone can, it's you."

✷

At three o'clock the next day, Amy waited for Scott to arrive with Spartan. Lou and Grandpa were out doing the grocery shopping, and it was Ty's day off, so Matt had come over to keep her company.

He kicked a stone down the drive as they waited for his brother. "Scott should get here soon," he said, glancing at his watch. "He said he'd be here before three."

"Yeah," Amy replied. Her heart was racing at the thought of seeing Spartan again. She was glad that Matt was there. He wasn't really into horses, and he couldn't fully understand how she was feeling, but just having him there made her feel better.

"Heard from Soraya lately?" Matt asked.

"I got a letter last week," Amy said. Soraya Martin was her best friend. She was away at a summer riding camp, and Amy was finding it hard not being able to speak to her on a regular basis. "She sounds like she's having fun."

"When's she coming back?"

"In three weeks," Amy replied. "I can't wait." She glanced at her watch nervously. Where was Scott? What was keeping him? He should have been here by now.

She walked over to the big gray horse in the end stall and stroked his nose. He nuzzled her affectionately. She smiled faintly. No matter how she was feeling, Pegasus always seemed to understand. He had been her father's horse — one of the finest show jumpers in the world. But a jumping accident in London twelve years before had left her father too injured to ever ride again, and Pegasus physically and emotionally damaged.

Amy kissed Pegasus's soft muzzle. It was through nursing Pegasus back to health that her mother had learned all about alternative therapies. Those methods had inspired her to move back to the United States and start Heartland — a horse sanctuary — after her marriage to Tim Fleming had broken up.

Matt walked over to Pegasus's stall. "It's twenty minutes past," he said with concern, looking at his watch. "I hope nothing's happened."

As Amy pulled away from Pegasus, her ears caught the faint chug of an engine coming up the drive. "That's probably him now," she said quickly.

A few seconds later, Scott's battered Jeep Cherokee came around the corner, a trailer swaying behind it. As it got closer, the sound of hooves crashing against metal could be heard. Matt and Amy exchanged nervous looks.

The Jeep stopped beside them. Scott cut the engine and jumped out. "What a journey!" he said. His face was strained as he nodded to the trailer. "I thought Spartan was going to burst out of the back at one point. He didn't stop kicking the whole way here."

There was a moment's silence, and then a high, whinnying scream rang out, full of rage and fury. Amy jumped as a hoof banged into the metal wall right next to her.

"Wow!" said Matt. "He sounds crazy!"

"He should calm down." Scott looked at Amy. "We'd better get him out. I'll go in and hold his halter while you two put the front ramp down." He disappeared through the side door. There was another series of thuds, and the trailer shook.

Amy's heart pounded in her chest as she moved around to unbolt the ramp. Any minute she'd see Spartan again. She remembered him as he had been the night she and her mom had rescued him — beautiful and trusting. And amazingly friendly considering he was a stallion and had been locked in a dark barn for days. He wasn't a stallion anymore. Scott had gelded him once it looked like he was going to recover and would be coming to Heartland to be rehabilitated and then rehomed. But even though he was no longer a stallion, he sounded wilder than ever.

"Let's go!" Scott shouted.

Amy and Matt let down the ramp, jumping aside just

in time as Spartan plunged forward with a screaming whinny.

"Easy now! Easy!" Scott shouted.

With a plunge, the horse clattered down the ramp. He stopped still and looked around at the fields and the fences, his bay coat gleaming with sweat, his eyes burning with fire.

Amy stood frozen. Spartan was unrecognizable. The trust and confidence that were in his eyes the first time she'd seen him had been replaced by fury and fear. Ugly scars stood out along his back and quarters. Guilt rushed through Amy as she looked at him. She felt a sudden desperate urge to turn and run away — far away.

Suddenly, Spartan's head whipped around as he caught her scent. With a sudden squeal of pure rage he lunged toward her, his mouth open, his ears flat against his head. Amy leaped back.

Scott struggled with the lead line to get the horse under control. "Are you all right?" he called anxiously to Amy.

"I'm fine," she replied breathlessly.

"We'd better get him into his stall," Scott said.

"I'll get the door," Matt said, edging cautiously past Spartan and then hurrying toward the barn.

Scott led Spartan after him. The horse sidestepped and shook his head as he jogged. He didn't seem to want to take his eyes off Amy, but Scott's voice and hand on his halter urged him onward.

Scott took him into the stall and secured the door behind him. "I'm sorry about what happened back there," he said to Amy. "I don't know what came over him. He's been difficult to handle, but he hasn't gone for anyone like that before."

"I guess it was probably just the shock of traveling in a trailer again," Amy reasoned. "It must have reminded him of the accident." She went to the door and looked over. She noticed Spartan stiffen as he saw her, and then, without warning, he plunged at the door, his snapping teeth missing her arm by inches.

"Whoa!" Scott shouted at the horse. Spartan shot to the back of his box again.

"Why'd he do that?" Matt asked Amy.

She looked quickly at Scott. "He hates me, doesn't he? He knows that it's my fault he was in the accident."

"He doesn't *hate* you," Scott said quickly. "Horses don't hold grudges. You know that. But he might associate you with the accident. He's probably attacking you because he's scared — scared that if he lets you get near, you'll put him through something similar again."

"So what's Amy supposed to do, Scott?" Matt asked, his voice full of concern.

"Rebuild his trust," Scott answered. His eyes met

Amy's. "It's going to be a long, slow process — but you've done it before."

*Yes*, Amy suddenly wanted to shout, *but not without Mom and never with a horse that was scared of me.*

Scott must have seen the doubt on her face. "You can do it, Amy — you might be the *only* person who can. If Spartan can come to trust and accept you, then he'll be able to trust anyone."

Amy swallowed. She would have to see Spartan every day, face his angry eyes, meet his resentment. She didn't know if she was up to it.

Scott studied her. "Look, if you really don't want to, then don't worry," he said. "I'll try to find somewhere else to take him."

Although Scott was hiding his disappointment, Amy knew that it wouldn't be easy to find someone else who would help Spartan. She swallowed. "No, I'll do it," she said.

Scott smiled. "That's great," he said, squeezing her shoulder. "It'll take time, Amy, but I know you can do it."

Amy glanced at Spartan's door, wishing she felt so sure.

# Chapter Two

Leaving Spartan to calm down, Scott asked if he could take a look at Sugarfoot.

"Sure," Amy said. Sugarfoot was a Shetland pony that she had been nursing back to health.

As they walked up the yard, past the turnout paddocks, Amy stopped to pat a handsome buckskin pony that was looking over the fence. "Hi, there," she said. Sundance snorted in reply and thrust his head affectionately into her chest.

"He's looking good," Scott said.

"Yeah," Amy nodded. She fed Sundance a couple of mints. Although it was Heartland's mission to find new homes for all of the horses they rescued, Sundance was by nature too unpredictable and tempermental to be rehomed, so he was one of the few permanent equine residents there. Badly behaved with everyone else, he utterly adored Amy. Whenever there was time, she entered him in hunter-jumper classes in local shows.

"How's Sugarfoot's recovery coming along?" Scott asked as they entered the twelve-stall barn on the north side of the yard.

"He's getting much better," Amy said. "He's eating well now."

Sugarfoot had been brought to Heartland when he was discovered in his stable. He'd had no food for two weeks after his elderly owner, Mrs. Bell, had died. When Sugarfoot had first arrived at Heartland he was grief stricken and had refused to eat. He became very ill with bronchopneumonia. He had been so sick that they'd thought they were going to lose him up until a week ago — when he had turned a corner and started to recover.

Sugarfoot was standing by his hayrack. He gave a low, welcoming nicker and walked up to say hello.

"He's looking great," Scott said, stroking the Shetland's thick flaxen mane. "What remedies have you been using?"

Amy listed the herbs and aromatherapy oils she had been treating Sugarfoot with. "Diluted neroli oil for massage, then garlic, fenugreek seed, and nettles in his feed," she said. "They seem to be helping him get his appetite back."

"It seems like he's almost back to his old self," Scott said approvingly. He checked Sugarfoot's breathing and heart rate. "He's improving fast."

"Well, it's really Lou who's been looking after him," Amy explained.

"Lou?" Scott questioned.

It had been a surprise to Amy as well. Ever since their father's accident and the subsequent breakup of their parents' marriage, Lou had refused to have anything to do with horses. Even when she had come to Heartland after their mom's death she had avoided any contact with the horses at first. However, Sugarfoot had captured her heart, and she'd been moved to help nurse him back to health.

"She spends as much time as she can with him," Amy said.

"How long is she planning on staying?" Matt asked.

"Well, she's told her boss at work that she won't be back until the fall," Amy said. She patted Sugarfoot gratefully. If it hadn't been for Sugarfoot, Lou would *already* have gone back to her high-powered banking job in Manhattan.

"What will you do when she does go back?" Scott asked.

Amy shrugged. She didn't want to think about it. When she went back to school in the fall they would just have to find the money to hire another stable hand — or else they'd have to reduce the number of horses. "Maybe she'll change her mind," Amy said optimistically.

"You think there's a chance?" Scott said in surprise. "I thought she was really into city life."

"She is," Amy admitted. Lou *was* into her job in a big way — her job and her apartment and Carl, her boyfriend. "But she seems to like it here, too. I don't know . . . she *might* stay."

Just then, there was the sound of a car pulling up outside the house. "That's probably Lou and Grandpa now," Amy said.

They headed toward the house. Jack Bartlett's station wagon was parked outside, and he and Lou were getting out.

"Hi!" Amy called.

"Hi," Grandpa replied. "Spartan's here, is he?"

"Yes. In the stall at the end," Amy said.

Curious, Grandpa and Lou walked over. Amy glanced at Matt, who was drinking a soda by the back door, and then hurried after them. "Don't go too close," she warned.

Grandpa stopped. "Why?" A look of concern flickered in his eyes as he studied her face. "He's not *dangerous*, is he?"

"No, no, of course not," Amy said quickly. "He's just a bit upset after the journey."

"Well, he's a good-looking horse," Grandpa commented, looking over the door. "A Morgan by the looks of him."

Scott turned to Amy. "Look, I'd better be going now. Call me if you need any advice, otherwise I'll drop by in a few days." He smiled at her. "You'll do a great job with him." He turned to Matt. "Do you want a lift?"

"Yeah, sure," Matt nodded.

They said their good-byes and then walked down to Scott's Cherokee. The engine coughed to life, and then with a belch of exhaust fumes, the Jeep and trailer trundled away.

✒

That night, Amy sat up in bed reading until late. She didn't want to fall asleep for fear of facing a nightmare again. Forcing her eyes to stay open, she read and read, but as the night wore on, the print started to blur, and at last her eyes closed.

She was in the dark. But where? Four wooden walls pressed in on her. It was some sort of barn. Rain drummed down onto the tin roof above, and the wind howled outside. Amy wasn't sure why she was in this dark, enclosed space, but she had an unrelenting desire to escape. Uneasily she moved toward the door. There was a sudden crash of thunder followed by a creak as the door slowly opened. Her heart raced.

"Mom!" Amy gasped, seeing Marion standing there, her hair soaked with rain and plastered to her head, a halter in hand.

"Easy," Marion soothed. She seemed to be talking to Amy. Then she turned to someone behind her. "Stand back a bit now," she said, putting a hand in her pocket and taking out a tin.

With the next fork of lightning the two silhouettes were lit up, and Amy recognized her own figure hovering behind her mom. Suddenly, she realized what was happening. Everything was like the night of the accident, but she was seeing the events through Spartan's eyes. She was seeing her mom and herself as Spartan had seen them. She could feel his fear, his bewilderment!

Her mom stepped toward her, holding her hand out. There was a clap of thunder, a moment of total blackness, and then the scene changed. The dream jumped ahead. Amy heard a metal clang as a door shut fast behind her, echoing ominously like a prison door. She realized she was now inside the trailer. She could hear the engine of the pickup starting and felt the trailer rock as it began to move.

Panic gripped Amy. She knew what was coming next. "Let me out!" she screamed. Her head was tied so she couldn't get loose. She lashed out at the metal walls, rocking the trailer, but to no avail. She was trapped. She couldn't see where they were, but she knew where they were going. The rain hammered relentlessly against the roof. There was the sound of the fierce wind and of creaking branches, and then she heard it. The spine-chilling, cannon-loud crack of a tree trunk breaking, the sound of squealing brakes, a bang, and then nothing.

❧

Amy opened her eyes and snapped her light on. She took in lungfuls of air, and her breathing gradually steadied. Her room seemed eerily quiet. Reaching out for her book, she opened it with shaking fingers. It was still dark outside and she was exhausted, but she couldn't face going back to sleep.

❧

The minutes dragged by until it was an acceptable time to get up. Amy met Lou down in the kitchen, and after grabbing a coffee and a muffin they went outside to feed the horses. The sky was a cloudless blue, and the early morning air was clear and cool.

"What a beautiful day!" Lou said. "You know, on mornings like this Manhattan seems totally unreal. Sometimes I can't imagine getting up and going to work in an office again."

Just then, the peace was shattered as Spartan put his head over his door and let out a piercing whistle at the sight of Amy. He half reared in his stall.

Lou gasped in alarm. "What's the matter with him?"

"It's me," Amy admitted. "He's scared of me because of the accident." She ran a hand through her hair. "Look, it might be best if you feed him. Or we could wait till Ty gets here."

"I'll do it. There's no point waiting for Ty," Lou said as they entered the feed room. "I wonder what Carl will think of it here," she contemplated, unscrewing the lid of the cod liver oil tin as Amy started adding heaping scoops of grain to the buckets. "He'll be here in a couple of days."

Amy had met Carl only once when she had been visiting Lou in Manhattan. He hadn't seemed at all interested in hearing about Heartland, and Amy wasn't sure how she felt about him.

"I can't imagine it," Lou mused. "I've never been with him in the country." She started to stack the feeds up. "Still, maybe he'll have some ideas for how this place could make money."

"Make money?" Amy repeated.

"Yes," Lou replied, obviously noticing the doubt on Amy's face. "Well, we're going to have to raise some more money somehow — even *you* can appreciate that, Amy. Without Mom it's going to be a struggle to persuade customers to bring their horses here. I know Nick Halliwell said he would bring us some business. . . ."

"And he has," Amy interrupted.

Nick Halliwell was a famous show jumper. He had recently brought one of his best horses to Heartland so Amy could cure its fear of being loaded into a trailer. Star had been the first problem horse that Amy had attempted to heal without her mom. Within two days the horse was going in and out of the trailer with no problem. Nick Halliwell had been very impressed with Amy's work and had promised to recommend Heartland to all his friends. And two new horses — Raisin and Topper — had already arrived to be treated.

"But we can't *rely* on him," Lou pointed out. "We have to try to raise our profile in other ways as well. I've had some ideas that I'm going to work on this afternoon. I know she did her best, but Mom really didn't run this place in the most economical way. We simply *have* to make more money." She picked up the buckets for the front stable. "It may mean a few changes, but I'm sure we will manage."

Amy headed up to the back barn with the other pile of buckets. *A few changes.* She bit her lip. She didn't want changes. She wanted everything to stay just the way it had been before Mom died.

Ty arrived at seven thirty. He and Amy began their normal morning routine — turning horses out, cleaning stalls, filling water buckets. As Amy worked she became aware of Spartan watching her. She didn't want to look at him, and yet her gaze seemed irresistibly drawn to his stall. Time after time she would glance over to see what she thought was fear in his eyes. Every time she walked anywhere near his stall, his ears flattened and he snapped at the air.

She saw Ty coming out of Pegasus's loose box and went over to talk with him. "What do you think about Spartan?" she asked, trying to sound casual as she tickled Pegasus's muzzle.

Ty bolted the door. "You really want to know?"

Amy nodded.

"Well, I'm not sure about him," Ty said seriously. "Watch yourself, Amy."

Amy surprised herself by jumping to Spartan's defense. "He's not *really* bad," she said quickly. "You should have seen him before the accident when Mom and I went to get him. He was so gentle."

"I don't know." Ty shook his head. "He's got a lot of distrust in his eyes. He's been through some awful stuff. I just want you to be careful."

"He'll settle in," Amy said uneasily, looking up at Ty. "He'll get better." She said the words automatically, feeling a desperate need to believe them herself. If Spartan didn't get better, what would it mean for her? She knew she wouldn't be able to deal with him being put down. It wasn't his fault he couldn't trust anyone. She *had* to make him better.

# Chapter Three

Amy was busy enough over the next few hours to keep her mind off Spartan. She brought Raisin, the younger of the two new show jumpers, out of the barn with a halter and longline on.

Raisin was a pretty, young chestnut who panicked and tried to bolt every time a rider attempted to mount her. In all other respects — being groomed, handled, and led — the mare was obedient and responsive. Amy was sure that her problem could be cured.

As she led the chestnut up to the circular ring by the turnout paddocks, Lou came jogging into the yard. "What are you doing with Raisin today?" she asked with interest.

"I'm going to join up with her," Amy said. Joining up was a way of establishing a relationship of trust and understanding with a horse. It was a technique Marion had taught Amy.

"May I watch?" Lou asked.

"Sure," Amy said.

When they reached the circular ring, Lou leaned against the fence. After shutting the gate behind them, Amy rubbed Raisin's forehead with the palm of her hand and then unclipped the longline. She tossed one end toward the horse's hindquarters. With a slight jump of surprise, Raisin trotted away. Moving quickly so that her shoulders were in line with Raisin's, Amy pitched the longline again. With a snort, the chestnut broke into a high-headed canter.

By keeping her shoulders square with Raisin's body and her eyes fixed on the mare's eyes, Amy urged the mare on. After seven circuits she stepped slightly into the horse's path, blocking her movement and sending her at a canter in the opposite direction.

"Look," she said to Lou after Raisin made a few more circuits. "See her ear?" Raisin's inside ear was pointing into the circle in Amy's direction. "It means she's ready."

She urged the mare to circle the ring a few more times, waiting patiently for the next signal. At last it came. Raisin slowed to a trot and started to lick and chew with her mouth. This was the way a horse showed that it wanted to be friends. Then came the final signal.

Raisin stretched out her head and neck so that her muzzle was almost on the floor.

In one swift movement, Amy turned her shoulders sideways so she wasn't facing the horse and dropped her eyes, concentrating entirely on Raisin and forgetting about Lou's steady gaze on her. Out of the corner of her eye she saw Raisin slow to a stop. The horse stared at Amy and then decisively walked into the middle of the circle up to Amy's back, stopping by her shoulder and snorting softly. It was the moment of the join up!

Amy slowly turned and rubbed Raisin's forehead. "Good girl," she murmured before walking away. Raisin's instinct told her that humans were predators, but now Amy was trying to tell Raisin that she wasn't a threat — by moving away with nonaggressive body language. For the join up to be a success, she wanted Raisin to voluntarily choose to be with her and to follow her. To Amy's delight, as she walked across the ring the young chestnut did exactly that — she followed, with her nose by Amy's shoulder, her warm breath on Amy's neck. When she was certain she had Raisin's trust, Amy stopped and rewarded her with another rub on the forehead.

"Now that we've got an understanding," Amy told Lou, "I can start working on getting her used to being ridden. She'll be much easier to handle now."

To prove her point, she ran her palms over Raisin's

back and then eased her weight onto her hands. Raisin didn't flinch. "See, Raisin, I'm not going to hurt you. You'll be just fine." Amy stroked her and gave her a pat. "That's enough for today," she said.

Lou's eyes shone as she opened the gate. "That was incredible!"

Amy smiled. She had watched her mom join up on numerous occasions and understood exactly how Lou was feeling. Mom always said that no matter how many times she did it, it never felt any less amazing.

"So, are you going to join up with Spartan?" Lou asked curiously as they led Raisin back to the barn.

Ty, who was walking past with a water bucket, stopped. "It would be crazy to try and join up now," he said, looking at Amy. "There's no telling what he might do."

"He's not *that* bad," Amy protested, but she knew deep down that Ty was right.

"He could be dangerous," Ty said, his dark eyes serious.

"He's not," Amy retorted, seeing the look of concern on her sister's face. She turned to Ty. "Look, relax. I wasn't thinking about joining up with him yet. He'd probably try to jump out of the ring at this point."

"Or worse," Ty said.

Amy ignored him. "I thought I'd just try to get him used to me first. Go into his stall, brush him." She swallowed. "I'm going to start this afternoon."

❧

After lunch, as Amy approached Spartan's stall, she realized that never before had she experienced such a reluctant feeling about working with a horse. Spartan stared warily at her, his head high, his long black forelock tumbling down over his handsome, dished face. Amy hesitated. Although she was nervous, her natural instinct was to walk straight up to his door. She needed to get close to him, to make him realize that he had nothing to fear.

She took a step forward.

Immediately, Spartan threw his head up and half reared. Amy stopped in her tracks, frozen by indecision.

*Maybe*, she thought, *if I just stand here, he'll calm down in a minute and let me get closer. But then, I might just make things worse.*

She waited, but Spartan didn't calm down. He paced from foot to foot, his head held high. After several long minutes, Amy fetched a chair from the tack room and placed it directly in front of the stall. Spartan moved ceaselessly, side to side, back and forth.

An hour passed. Amy stood up and tried to move the chair a little closer, but Spartan reared violently. Amy decided to give him a break — maybe she'd have more luck tomorrow. As she returned the chair to the tack room, she couldn't help worrying that she wouldn't have any luck at all. *Maybe I should just call Scott and tell him that this isn't going to work,* she thought. *But how can I, when he has so much faith in me?*

As she walked back to the stable block, Spartan was looking out over his door. She paused, downwind from him. He was looking out across the fields, unaware of her. His ears were pricked forward, and for one fleeting moment she saw the beautiful, intelligent horse that he had been before the accident.

Amy stepped forward. Spartan heard her footstep and swung his head around. His eyes fixed on her, and in that moment a terrible knowledge seemed to flow between them — a shared memory of that horrific night. With a snort, Spartan plunged back into his stall.

Amy stood rooted to the spot. Suddenly, she knew that she wasn't going to call Scott — she couldn't. Like it or not, she and Spartan were bound together. However much he hated her, she was the only one who could understand what he had been through. She was the only one who could make things OK again.

&#x9E;

That evening, while Amy and Lou were cleaning up after supper, the phone rang. Amy answered it and then handed it to Lou. "It's for you. It's Carl."

Lou took the phone eagerly. "Carl!"

Amy switched the TV on and collapsed into the easy

chair. In the background she heard Lou tell Carl every-thing that had been going on. After a bit there was a pause. "Yes, I miss you, too," Lou said into the phone. "I can't wait to see you again. Only two more days now."

Amy rolled her eyes.

Then Lou's tone changed slightly. "I can't come back yet. You know I'm needed here, Carl." There was a pause, and then her voice took on just the faintest tinge of irritation. "I don't know when," she said. "Yes, I know I said the end of the summer but . . ." She broke off. "Of course, I want to be with you, but for now I have to stay at Heartland." She looked around and saw Amy watch-ing her. She lowered her voice. "Look, we can talk about this when you get here."

Amy turned back to the television.

"How's Carl?" Grandpa asked as Lou put the phone down.

"Fine, he's . . ."

"Hey, look! I don't believe it!" Amy sat up suddenly in her chair, interrupting Lou. "There's a commercial for Green Briar on TV!"

Green Briar was a large boarding and show-jumping stable not far from Heartland. Val Grant, Green Briar's owner, was standing in front of a newly painted eighteen-stall barn, smiling broadly at the camera.

Grandpa and Lou came over and stood behind the easy chair.

"Want a perfect pony?" the voice-over on the TV asked as the camera shot changed to show a couple of beautiful ponies cantering around a course of jumps. "A pony that'll win you lots of ribbons?"

Amy scowled. She knew all about the forceful techniques that Val Grant used to make her ponies canter so correctly, heads poised, hooves snapping up precisely as they cleared a jump.

The camera zoomed in closer on one of the riders. "It's Ashley!" Amy exclaimed.

Ashley Grant was fifteen, and she and Amy were in the same class at high school. The large pony she was riding cantered smoothly toward a jump. Ashley's immaculate breeches clung to her slim legs, her sleek blond hair was pulled back neatly in a bun under her hunt cap, and her face was beautifully made up. Her pony jumped the fence perfectly, and she brought it to a halt and smiled straight into the camera.

"If you've ever dreamed of owning a perfect pony," the voice said as the camera cut to a shot of Val Grant petting a pony with a blue ribbon fluttering on his bridle, "then come to Green Briar. The place where dreams really *can* come true."

"Gross!" Amy exclaimed as the music faded out and the next commercial came on. She turned to Grandpa and Lou indignantly. "The whole thing's just aimed at people who want ribbon-winning, push-button ponies!"

Grandpa nodded in agreement, but Lou was looking at the TV thoughtfully. "You know, that's not a bad idea — making a commercial," she said. "Maybe we should consider it. Speaking of which . . ." She snapped off the TV. "Grandpa, Amy, it's time I told you about the plans I've been making for Heartland."

"Ah, yes, your plans to make us more profitable," Grandpa said, looking at the blank TV screen.

"Yes," Lou said briskly. "Now don't look at me like that, Amy," she said, seeing her sister's face cloud over. "When it comes to business, I know what I'm talking about. It's what I'm good at." She reached for a pile of papers. "First of all," she said, "it's obvious that we need better cash flow. Before the winter, the roof on the barn is going to need repairs and there'll be other expenses — blankets, extra hay, and straw. In addition, I feel that we need to maximize Heartland's potential."

"You sound like you're in a business meeting, Lou," Amy protested. "We're talking about Heartland — it's a horse sanctuary."

"But this place *is* a business." Before Amy had a chance to say anything more, Lou continued, "We have to think of it that way. Now, my first goal is to raise money for the winter. I thought that we could hold a barn dance."

"A barn dance?" Jack Bartlett questioned.

"Don't look like that, Grandpa," Lou chided. "A dance

is an ideal way to raise money. We can get a band, provide food and drinks, and then charge for the tickets and hold a raffle. This place is plenty big enough," she said.

"But who would come?" Amy blurted out.

"Mom's friends," Lou said. "It would be the ideal opportunity to invite them up here. I think they've been staying away to give us enough time. . . ." She trailed off for a moment. "It would be a way of breaking the ice — of showing them that we don't want them to stay away anymore. And it's a cause they'd support."

"But, Lou, are you sure it would work?" Jack Bartlett ran a hand through his hair. "It sounds expensive — a band, food, prizes for the raffle. How would we pay for all that?"

"Well, there would be the money from the tickets, and we could ask people to help out and donate things. Everyone has always been willing to help Heartland in the past, haven't they?" Grandpa nodded. "Well, they will again," Lou said. "The whole idea is that the event will cost us very little, but we'll make a substantial amount of money."

"What if people don't come?" Amy said. She was finding it hard to imagine their family's friends coming to a dance where they had to pay for tickets.

"But they will! It's for a good cause," Lou insisted. She looked around. "Well, what do you say?"

"OK, I guess," Grandpa said tentatively.

"Great!" Lou said. "I'll start organizing it — we'll aim to have it in two or three weeks. The sooner the better."

"Two weeks!" Amy said.

Lou waved a hand. "That gives me enough time, no problem. Carl will help out when he gets here. I'll start calling around right away."

Amy frowned. She didn't have a good feeling about this dance. It just didn't seem right to her.

Lou straightened her papers. Amy noticed that, for the first time in ages, she looked in her element — like she was excited and knew exactly what to do next. "Now let's look at some ways of increasing Heartland's profits. Obviously, the bulk of our income is from the paying horses — the nonresidents whose owners bring them here to have their problems solved. I think we need to market ourselves more effectively in order to get the maximum number of paying customers." She pulled out a piece of paper. "So, I propose that we have some sort of brochure that we can distribute in tack shops, to feed merchants — basically anywhere that horsey people go. Take a look at this outline."

Amy could see that the piece of paper she was holding was split into three sections. There was a column with the title HEARTLAND in big letters with suggestions for several photographs. The next column described Heartland's work, with quotes from a recent magazine article and AS RECOMMENDED BY NICK HALLIWELL in large letters across the top of it, and the final section detailed the services Heartland offered and the fees that were charged. Amy's heart sank. Lou just didn't understand what Heartland was about. Mom had never given estimates for how much treatments would cost! She had always had a flexible system for charging people, avoiding set fees because she believed that every horse was an individual and needed a different approach. A couple of lines on the page caught Amy's eye:

> *At Heartland we make a unique offer — for $50 we will assess your horse's needs and provide a detailed written evaluation.*

"No," Amy said, shaking her head. "We can't do this." She pointed at the offending sentence.

"What's the matter?" Lou asked.

"We're not going to start evaluating horses and charging people for it. No way!"

"Why not?" Lou said. "It's perfectly normal. If you want someone to do some work for you, you have to get a quote first and then decide whether you want to pursue it."

"But how can we?" Amy exclaimed. "You can't tell

how long a horse is going to take to be cured until you start working with it — and even then you may have setbacks, or things might not go as planned. Mom *never* charged people until after treatment was complete."

"People expect a quote," Lou said. "It's a more professional approach."

"Well, I'm not doing it!" Amy interrupted. "I don't want to change things. Everything worked just fine for Mom."

"Everything could have worked *better*," Lou said. She shook her head, looking upset. "Amy, I'm only trying to help. We don't *have* to carry on doing things exactly the way Mom did. We can make changes to make things easier for ourselves."

"No, we can't!" Amy said, her voice rising as panic took hold of her. She didn't want any changes. She didn't even know how to give a quote before treatment. She wanted things to stay just the way Mom had left them. "You can forget it, Lou! Forget this whole stupid brochure idea!" She jumped to her feet.

"Come on, Amy," Grandpa suggested. "Sit down, and let's discuss it calmly."

"No!" Amy said. She stormed to the door and slammed it behind her.

Fighting a tide of anxiety, she hurried up to her bedroom. She couldn't let Lou change things! That just couldn't happen!

Opening her door, she immediately focused on the photograph of her mom on her dressing table. She walked over and picked it up. "Oh, Mom," she whispered desperately. "Why aren't you here?"

# Chapter Four

The next morning the mood in the kitchen was tense. Amy had woken up with nightmares again. She felt groggy from the lack of sleep and depressed by the argument of the day before. She scowled at Lou as she sat down at the table.

"Can you pass the milk, please?" Lou asked.

Amy handed her the carton, banging it down on the table. She got up again, brushing past Lou to get to the teapot.

"Amy!" Lou said angrily as Amy knocked her arm.

"Oh, come on, you two," Jack Bartlett said with a sigh. "How about a compromise?" He paused. "We'll still consider the brochure idea, Lou, but maybe you can rework it and then discuss it again with Amy."

"But it doesn't need reworking, Grandpa!" Lou protested. "I really do think it's fine as it is . . ."

"Compromise," Grandpa said firmly.

"OK," Lou sighed. "I'll take another look at it." She looked at Amy. "But the dance *is* going ahead."

Grandpa nodded. "Yes. The dance can go ahead, and Amy and I will give you all the help you need." He threw Amy a warning glance as she opened her mouth to object. "Won't we, Amy?"

"I guess," she muttered.

"Good," said Grandpa with a smile. "Now can we just get along and be civilized with one another, *please*?"

🙢

In the middle of the morning, Scott's old Cherokee came chugging up the drive. Amy hurried across the yard to meet him. "Hey," he said to her, getting out. "I was just passing and thought I'd stop by."

Lou was walking across the yard with an armful of fresh grass. She stopped and waited for them to catch up. "Hello, Scott."

Scott smiled, looking at the grass in her arms. "For Sugarfoot?"

"Yes," Lou said. "I gave him some yesterday, and he loved it. Do you want to see him?"

Scott joined her. As they walked toward the north

barn, Amy overheard Lou telling him about her plans for the barn dance.

"That sounds great!" Scott said, obviously impressed. "You can put me down for a ticket! I'll spread the word, too. After all, it's for a good cause."

"That's wonderful!" Lou said, her eyes shining. "Thanks, Scott."

Amy felt surprised — she wouldn't have thought Scott would be interested in something like a dance. Maybe she was just being unreasonable and it *was* a good idea after all. Yawning, she went into the tack room.

Ty was busy cleaning a bridle. He looked up as Amy grabbed a grooming bucket. "Who are you going to groom?"

"Spartan," Amy said.

"Are you sure?" Ty asked.

"It's now or never," Amy said resolutely.

She didn't even hesitate when she came to Spartan's stall. As she opened the door, he plunged forward. But Amy was quicker. She snatched his halter, quickly snapping a lead rope onto one of the rings. Feeling her hand near his face, Spartan panicked. He rose up on his back legs, and his front hooves came crashing down, but Amy held on, staying close beside him and moving her free hand to his head the second his hooves hit the ground. Eyes rolling, Spartan reluctantly submitted to the control of the halter and rope but he didn't relax.

"Easy now," Amy soothed, picking up a grooming brush.

Spartan started in alarm. His body language told her he didn't want her in his stall. He didn't want her holding his head, and he didn't want her trying to brush him. With determination, Amy lifted the brush to his coat. He flinched as if she had hit him.

Amy sighed. She knew she should keep trying to groom Spartan, be firm but kind with him, keep persisting, but she just couldn't bear to make him more nervous and afraid than he already was. She put the brush back in the bucket. Maybe she would just take him out to graze instead. That might help him feel more at home.

Keeping a watchful eye on him, she led him out of his stall and over to a large patch of grass in front of the house. He snorted, moving beside her with high, nervous steps. Amy stopped him where the grass was thickest, but he didn't lower his neck. Instead, he stood with every muscle tensed and his eyes fixed on her.

Ty came over.

"I was hoping he might relax and eat a little grass," Amy explained. "But it doesn't look like he's going to."

"Do you want me to hold him?" Ty offered.

"OK," Amy said.

Ty took the lead rope.

Once Spartan was satisfied that Amy was at a safe distance, he put his head down and jerkily started to snatch at the grass. Amy wiped the sweat off her forehead with the back of her hand.

Ty looked over. "Just give it time," he said quietly.

Amy nodded. Ty always seemed to understand how she was feeling when it came to horses. They worked really well together. Standing in silence, they watched Spartan graze.

After a while, Scott came around the barn with Lou. "How's Spartan doing?" he asked, looking at the bay horse.

Amy wondered what to say. How could she admit to Scott that she wasn't making any progress? What would he think? "He's OK," she said quickly.

"Good," Scott smiled. "Well, keep up the hard work."

As he turned and walked off toward his Cherokee, Amy caught Ty giving her a puzzled look, but to her relief he didn't say anything. She watched Scott drive away and then sighed. "I'd better put Spartan back in his stall now," she said. "We've still got a lot to do."

"Sure," Ty replied.

Amy took the lead rope from him, and Spartan pulled back in alarm. "Easy now," Amy soothed, but the horse threw his head up wildly. Amy moved in closer to him and tightened her grip. "Walk on," she said, clicking her tongue.

As Spartan reluctantly stepped forward beside her, Amy could sense fear pulsating through every muscle and nerve in his body.

Lou came over as Ty opened Spartan's stall door for Amy. "How is he?" she asked, looking apprehensively at the bay horse.

"Fine," Amy said curtly. She led Spartan into his stall and automatically unclipped his lead rope.

Free at last, he threw himself toward Amy, the full force of his body slamming into her and knocking her against the wall. She stumbled and heard Lou scream and Ty shout out her name as Spartan swung his hindquarters toward her. But Amy acted quickly. Scrambling to her feet, she flung herself toward his head, her fingers fumbling for the halter. Grasping the leather, she forced Spartan to lower his head and backed him into a corner until he was under control again. For a moment she stood there, clutching his halter, her heart pounding.

"Amy! Get out of the stall!" Lou cried.

Amy looked around to see Lou and Ty staring at her in shock.

Not wanting to turn her back on him, she led Spartan over to the door, only letting go of him when she could slip out safely. Then she let out a shaky breath.

Lou grabbed her by the shoulders. "Amy! What were you thinking? You could have been badly hurt."

"It was nothing." Amy pulled away, her hands still trembling slightly. She glanced back at the stall, not wanting either of them to blame Spartan. "It was stupid of me. I should never have unclipped his lead like that."

"But he tried to kick you!" Lou exclaimed.

"But he didn't," Amy protested. She shook her head, angry at herself. "I should have been more careful."

"More careful!" Lou exclaimed. "That horse is dangerous, Amy! He might need to be put down."

"What?" Amy gasped.

"He's not safe," Lou stated emphatically.

Anger surged through Amy. "What would you know?" she cried, drawing herself up. "You're an expert all of a sudden, are you?" She saw Lou's face stiffen but was too upset to stop herself. "You don't know what you're talking about, Lou! You don't know what he's been through," she shouted. "Just stay out of it!"

Lou went pale and then turned swiftly away.

There was a moment's pause, then Ty cleared his throat. "Amy, I hate to say it, but she has a point."

Amy swung around. "She shouldn't have said that!"

"She's just concerned about you," Ty said. "I am, too. I've never seen a horse turn on anyone like that."

Amy felt her cheeks flame with guilt and humiliation.

"You're not making things any better." Amy dropped her eyes to the ground and sighed. "Just keep out of it, Ty," she said under her breath.

"OK," Ty said shortly. "If that's how you feel, you're on your own." He turned and walked off.

As Amy watched him disappear out of sight, her temper suddenly faded as quickly as it had flared up. "*Great*," she muttered, throwing down the lead rope. "Just great!"

From the end of the row of stalls there was a snort. Amy looked around and saw Pegasus watching her. "Oh, Pegasus," she groaned, walking over. Pegasus nuzzled her hair. Amy stroked his neck and felt her flurry of emotions gradually ebb. She sighed. She knew what she had to do.

Taking a deep breath, she walked across the yard. Ty was sweeping the aisle near the muck heap. Hearing her footsteps, he glanced up. But when he saw it was Amy, he concentrated on his sweeping again.

"I'm sorry, Ty," Amy said.

Ty leaned on the yard broom and looked at her.

"I shouldn't have said those things," Amy continued. "I — I just lost it."

"It's OK," Ty said with a shrug.

"It's not," Amy said quickly. "I didn't mean them." She rubbed her forehead. "Everything's just getting to me. I haven't been sleeping well. I'm sorry, Ty — really I am."

Ty's face softened. "Look, forget it."

Amy breathed a sigh of relief. She hated it when Ty was mad at her. "Thanks," she said gratefully.

He picked up the broom again. "So are you going to apologize to Lou?"

"After she said those things about Spartan?" Amy protested. "She doesn't know what she's talking about."

Ty shrugged. "Maybe not." He glanced up. "But she does care about you, and that's why she said those things, Amy."

"I don't think so!" she said, reading his expression. "I am *not* going to apologize to her." She saw Ty's eyebrows raise. "I don't want her to think putting Spartan down is even an option!"

# Chapter Five

As the hours passed, Amy began to feel guilty about the way she had treated Lou — but she still couldn't bring herself to apologize. Every time she thought about Spartan being put down she felt like she wanted to be sick.

Amy avoided going into the farmhouse all day until she couldn't put it off any longer. She said good night to the horses and walked reluctantly to the back door.

Lou was setting the table.

As Amy walked in and their eyes met, she turned away and kicked off her sneakers. She waited for her sister to tell her to put them away, but Lou didn't say a word.

Amy poured some juice from the refrigerator and glanced across at Lou, who was placing the three sets of knives and forks down, each metal piece making a dull thud against the table. Her face was pale, her mouth rigid.

Amy suddenly couldn't bear the atmosphere any longer. "Lou . . ."

Lou looked up at her.

"I shouldn't have said those things," Amy said quickly. "I'm sorry. I didn't mean to hurt you."

Lou's face softened. "Oh, Amy," she said, stepping forward. "I was just so worried about you —"

Lou broke off quickly as Jack Bartlett came into the kitchen.

"Hi, honey," he said to Amy. Then he frowned. "I hear you had a bit of a problem with Spartan today."

Amy's eyes shot to Lou, who looked away — her cheeks flushing.

"Amy?" her grandpa prompted.

"Well, not really," Amy lied desperately, her mind racing. Why had Lou told Grandpa? If he thought Spartan was dangerous he would stop her from working with him. "He was kind of excitable," she said quickly. "But nothing really bad."

"He tried to attack you, Amy!" Lou said.

"He did not!" Amy exclaimed. "You're exaggerating!"

"You know I'm not!" Lou yelled back at her.

"That's enough!" Grandpa shouted, slamming his fist down on the kitchen table.

Amy and Lou glared at each other.

Jack looked from one granddaughter to the other. "If he's that dangerous, Amy . . ."

"He isn't!" Amy interrupted. "Grandpa, he just needs help!"

Her grandpa looked at her for a moment as if he was going to say something, and then to Amy's relief he let the matter drop and turned to deal with the stew bubbling on the top of the stove. Amy scowled at Lou and stomped past her to go get changed.

The next morning, when Amy came downstairs, Lou was busy making out an invitation list for the dance.

"Morning, Grandpa," Amy yawned, shaking out a couple of aspirin from a bottle in the cabinet. She had been awake since four o'clock, and her head throbbed.

"Are you OK?" Jack asked, looking at her in concern.

Amy nodded.

Lou looked up from her notepad. "We need to decide on the food for the dance," she declared. "I thought we might have a barbecue. Then all we need to do is get a load of steaks, some chicken, and some corn on the cob, and that's most of the food done. What do you think?"

"Sounds great," Grandpa said. He turned. "What do you think, Amy?"

Amy shrugged. "Whatever."

"That leaves the desserts." Lou looked straight at Amy.

"But I won't bother telling you about those. You don't seem to be the least bit interested in trying to save Heartland."

"Stop it!" Grandpa said. "This arguing has gone on long enough." He looked from one to the other. "Now, listen. I know you both are under a huge amount of pressure, but I don't want you taking it out on each other. You are both too important to me. How about we take a trip to the movies on Sunday? It would do us all some good to get out for the day, and I'd like to see you two enjoy being together for a change. What do you say?"

"Sure," Amy shrugged.

"Fine," Lou said flippantly. "Carl might still be here, so he can come, too."

"Oh, great," Amy muttered under her breath.

Lou looked at her sharply. "What?"

Amy caught Grandpa's warning look. "Nothing," she sighed. She walked to the door. "I'm going to feed the horses."

🕊

Right after breakfast, Lou set off to pick up Carl from the airport. After finishing the stalls with Ty, Amy went to see Spartan. She was attempting to groom him when a shadow fell across the door. Amy turned around.

Her grandpa was standing there. "Hey," he said.

"Hi," Amy said, her heart sinking. She was worried that Spartan might act up in front of her grandpa.

To her horror, he unbolted the door and came in. Spartan instinctively shrank back.

"It's OK," Amy murmured, stroking his neck.

But Spartan lashed out with his front hoof. The whites of his eyes flashed as he looked from Amy to her grandfather and back to her.

"Why did he do that?" Grandpa asked with a frown.

"He doesn't like me touching him," Amy said quietly.

Jack shook his head, looking at Spartan's flattened ears and rolling eyes. "I don't have a good feeling about him, Amy."

"He'll be fine," Amy insisted. "He's just traumatized. I'm going to help him. I'm going to make him better."

Her grandpa sighed. "Amy, honey, not every horse can be helped, even your mom used to admit that," he said, coming up close. "Sometimes, as hard as it is, it's best to just accept that there isn't — "

"No," Amy interrupted him, not wanting to hear what she knew he was going to say. She took a step toward her grandfather, preparing to plead her case. But with Amy's back turned, Spartan suddenly jerked his neck upward. Amy jumped away as she saw his head swing around. But Grandpa didn't react so fast. Spartan's teeth sank into his bare arm.

Amy's grandfather let out a yell of pain. Slowed by

shock, Amy grabbed at Spartan's halter, but it was too late.

"My arm!" Grandpa exclaimed. Spartan's teeth had left an ugly red welt on the skin.

"Grandpa, I'm sorry!" Amy gasped. Her eyes shot to Spartan. He was standing, unrepentant, with his ears still back. She followed her grandpa as he hurriedly let himself out of the stall. "It was a mistake," she said, her eyes filling with tears. "He didn't mean it." Behind her, Spartan's hooves crashed into the wall of his stall. "Please, Grandpa, he really didn't. He's just afraid."

But Jack Bartlett was silent as he strode down to the house, holding his arm. In the kitchen, Amy watched as he opened the first aid kit and cleansed the bite. She felt horribly guilty. "I'll get some arnica cream," she offered, desperate to find something she could do to help. "It will help reduce the bruising."

Amy hurried to the main barn and searched the cabinet in the feed room where all the natural remedies were kept. She returned to the house with the cream.

Grandpa applied it to his arm. His face was serious. As he screwed the top back on the jar he looked directly at Amy, speaking quietly but firmly. "This is a problem, Amy. He's going to really hurt somebody one of these days."

Amy swallowed. "He won't, Grandpa. He's going to get better. He just needs more time."

"I'd like to believe you, but I can't." Grandpa sighed. "I think . . ." But before he could say what he thought there was the sound of a car stopping outside the house.

Amy looked out of the window. "It's Lou and Carl!" Relief flooded through her as the car doors opened. She knew their arrival would distract Grandpa for the meantime.

"We'll talk about this later," Grandpa said, heading toward the door.

Carl was standing by the car looking around, his dark hair immaculate, his eyes hidden by designer sunglasses. To Amy's surprise he was wearing jeans, a leather belt with a big buckle, and sturdy boots. For some reason she had expected him to be wearing a suit like the one she had seen him in before. She took a longer look at his clothes — they looked new and expensive, but he'd obviously made an effort to dress casually.

Lou came around the front of the car. "You remember Grandpa and Amy, don't you, Carl?" she said happily.

"Of course I do." Carl smiled at Amy and then stepped forward holding out his hand to Grandpa. "Pleased to meet you again, Jack."

"Did you have a good flight?" Jack Bartlett asked.

Carl nodded. "Not bad." He looked around. "This place is great."

Jack smiled. "Well, we like it. Why don't you bring your stuff in, and Lou can show you around."

"Yeah, sure." Pulling out a green-and-tan overnight bag from the back of the car, he slung it over his shoulder and followed Grandpa and Lou into the house.

Amy didn't go with them. She was feeling confused. Carl actually seemed pretty nice. It wasn't how she remembered him at all. She walked up to Pegasus's box and stroked him thoughtfully.

After a bit, Carl and Lou came out of the house. "This is Pegasus," Lou said as they got close. "He was Daddy's horse. He was one of the top show jumpers in the world . . . before the accident." Carl stepped toward the horse. "He can be a bit nervous around strangers," Lou warned quickly. "You should be careful how you approach him."

Carl laughed confidently. "I know how to approach a horse. I used to spend hours playing with my cousin's pony when we were kids. Hello, big fella!" he said, his hand reaching out to pat Pegasus firmly on the forehead. "How you doing?"

Alarmed by the sudden movement around his head, Pegasus shot backward into his stall with a snort.

"Hey!" Carl exclaimed, looking startled.

Amy frowned. "You need to be a little more gentle when you approach a horse for the first time. Some of the horses here have been through a lot and are very skittish," Amy tried to explain politely.

"All I did was pet him," Carl said defensively. "That horse is just bad-tempered."

*How would you like it if a stranger marched up to you and slapped you between the eyes?* Amy wanted to ask Carl, but she held back.

Carl turned to Lou. "So, what can I do to help out? How about I give that horse a good brushing — he looks dirty." He walked toward Spartan. "Hi there, boy!"

Spartan snaked his head forward.

"I think we'll leave Spartan alone," Lou said, grabbing Carl's arm and steering him away. "But there's a pony in the other barn that I want you to meet."

"Take me to him," Carl said. "Just tell me how I can help."

Lou looked at Amy. "We'll do that, OK? We'll be up with Sugarfoot."

Amy nodded. As she watched them walk up the yard toward the back barn, she heard Carl say, "Oh, boy, this takes me back." She frowned to herself. Carl obviously didn't know anything about horses, so why was he pretending he did?

&#x1f336;

That afternoon, Matt called. "Hi. How are you doing?"

"OK," Amy told him. "Carl's here."

"Oh, how's that going?" Matt asked.

Amy frowned. "I'm not sure. He really doesn't know anything about horses, but he's acting like he does. I think he's just trying to impress Lou."

"What's wrong with that?" Matt said, sounding mystified.

"I don't know . . ." Amy struggled to explain. "It's just that he's sort of trying too hard."

"Yeah," Matt said, not sounding like he understood. He paused. "Do you want to go and see a movie this week?"

Amy sighed. "I can't. It's really busy around this place with Carl here and Lou trying to get everything ready for the dance. Carl's taking us out for dinner tonight. But why don't you come by sometime?"

"Sure, OK," Matt said. "I'll see you soon."

As Amy put the phone down, the kitchen door opened. Lou and Carl came in, hand in hand. "Hi!" Lou said, her eyes shining. "I was hoping you'd be here. Carl's had some great ideas to make Heartland more profitable."

"What kind of ideas?" Amy said.

Carl sat down. "Just ways to help this place make money." He put his arms around Lou's waist and pulled her close.

Lou giggled and, bending down, kissed the top of his head. "It's great to have you here," she said to him.

Amy made a face and headed toward the door.

"Don't you want to hear what we have to say?" Lou

said, sounding hurt. "We thought that there could be an adopt-a-horse campaign. You know, people pay a certain amount and get a photo of a horse and a newsletter?"

Almost immediately, Amy shook her head. "It wouldn't work. We rehome all the horses we can. We don't have enough permanent residents for something like that."

"Oh," Lou said, the sparkle fading from her eyes.

"I mean, it's a good idea, but just not for us. I'm going back out to the yard, OK?" Amy said quickly, turning away to avoid any further discussion.

Over dinner in the restaurant, Lou and Carl told Grandpa and Amy about the other ideas they had come up with. Jack listened and nodded while Amy felt the tension rising inside her, but she tried to suppress it. Lou was obviously really happy having Carl around, and Amy didn't want to ruin the evening. She was even beginning to think that maybe she should try to like Carl for Lou's sake. But when Lou explained Carl's suggestion of limiting the number of stalls kept for rescue horses to five, and using all the other stalls for horses whose owners paid to have them cured, Amy couldn't restrain herself any longer.

"What?" she exclaimed loudly. Some of the other people in the restaurant looked over. Amy lowered her voice. "What are you thinking, Lou?"

"It makes sense," Lou said. "The paying horses would

support the cost of looking after the rescued horses, and we'd make a profit."

"We're not reducing the number of rescue horses!" Amy said. "In fact, we're not making any changes." Her throat felt tight. She thought about her mom's devotion to saving horses and how that was always her first priority. "Everything's got to stay just as Mom left it. No changes." Her head was aching. She saw Grandpa staring at her. He looked like he was about to say something. "No changes!" she repeated. Suddenly, she couldn't bear to be at the table any longer. She got to her feet and hurried to the rest room. She was relieved it was empty.

Amy looked at herself in the mirror. Her face was pale, her gray eyes were ringed with purple shadows from lack of sleep. Thoughts whirled around in her head — Lou and Carl, Spartan, changes to Heartland, Mom . . .

Shutting her eyes, she leaned her forehead against the cold mirror, desperately wishing she could be somewhere — anywhere — else.

As always, the nightmares came back that night. The creaking of the trees and the rain, the wind and the thunder ringing in her ears, and the sight of the tree steadily falling. When Amy switched on the light it was three thirty in the morning. She sat up, waiting for the feeling of panic to subside.

Taking a deep breath, she picked up a magazine from the floor. Pulling the blankets around her, she started leafing through it. She had been reading for about half an hour when her bedroom door creaked open. She glanced up. Grandpa was standing in the doorway, looking concerned.

"Amy?" he said in a low voice. "It's four o'clock in the morning. What's your light doing on?"

"I — I couldn't sleep," she said.

His face softened, and he came and sat down beside her. "Did you have that nightmare again?"

Amy nodded.

Jack looked at her for a moment and then stroked her hair. "Nighttime is always the worst, even without the dreams, isn't it?" he said softly. "I have nights when I lie awake wondering why I didn't stop you and your mom from going out in that storm. Those moments of that day just keep repeating in my mind."

Amy stared at him in surprise. "But it wasn't *your* fault, Grandpa!"

"I know," he said. "Deep down, I know that *nothing* could have stopped your mom going out that night once she'd decided to — just as nothing could have made her go if she didn't want to. But grief's like that." His eyes searched Amy's. "You always feel you could have done more. You always blame yourself."

Amy swallowed as Grandpa leaned over and hugged her. "It *will* get easier in time, honey," he said. "I promise you it will." He cradled her in his arms, rocking her back and forth.

Amy shut her eyes tightly. Her throat ached with unshed tears. *Was he right?* She knew he had no reason to blame himself, but did she? She had pleaded with Mom to go out that night. She wanted to save Spartan. But her grandpa's words ran around in her head: *Nothing could have made your mom go if she didn't want to.* She wished desperately that she could believe those words, *really* believe them.

❧

Although Carl had only planned to come for an overnight visit, he decided to stay the following day as well. By the evening, Amy was longing for him to go. As far as she was concerned, his interest in everything about Heartland was obviously just an act. Amy couldn't believe that Lou didn't see through it, but Lou seemed oblivious; she was delighted to have someone around who would take her ideas seriously for a change.

When Amy came in from finishing with the horses for the night she found Carl and Lou in the kitchen, dressed up as if ready to go out. "Put your shoes away," Lou automatically reminded her.

Stubbornly, Amy kicked her sneakers into a corner. She was tired and didn't want to hear Lou's nagging. "We need some more feed, Lou," she said abruptly.

"I've ordered some," Lou said. "It's arriving on Monday."

Amy looked at her in surprise. "But McCullochs doesn't deliver on Monday."

"We're not using McCullochs anymore," Lou said. "They're really expensive. Carl and I were looking into it this afternoon. Rathmores makes an alfalfa cube for half the price, so I think it's best to use them in the future."

Amy stared at her in disbelief. "You what?" she asked.

"I decided that we should use Rathmores," Lou repeated. "They're delivering on Monday."

"It's a good idea," Carl said. "It'll be more economical."

"No, it won't!" Amy exclaimed. "You'll have to cancel the order, Lou. Rathmores' food is second-rate. Mom always made a big deal about it. We'd have to use twice as much of their feed! We won't save money, and the horses' health will suffer because their food isn't as high a quality. Not to mention the problems it would cause for the horses that have trouble digesting. They'll be far more likely to colic and to have allergic reactions. It's just not good feed."

"I had no idea," Lou said, her face suddenly falling.

"I would have told you if you had asked," Amy said in frustration.

"It seemed like such a good idea," Lou said defensively. "Anyway, you never have the time to listen to me, Amy! You just go on about how things can't change."

"Can't you can see why?" Amy exploded. "There's too much to do around here, and you can't even help by doing something as easy as ordering feed!"

🙰

A little later, she heard the sound of the back door opening and, looking out of her bedroom window, saw Lou and Carl walking toward Lou's car. They were laughing together. Amy suddenly realized that she hadn't seen Lou laugh like that in ages. Doubt flickered in her mind. Was she wrong to dislike Carl so much? He obviously made Lou happy.

Amy struggled with her thoughts as she watched them get into the car. She wanted Lou to be happy, but she just couldn't repress the uncomfortable feelings she had about Carl. And she couldn't stop herself from yelling at Lou whenever she tried to change Heartland. She sighed. Maybe she should make more of an effort. After all, she wanted Lou to stay at Heartland more than just about anything. Even if she had to learn to compromise — even if she had to be nicer to Carl. She sighed again. It would not be easy, but she'd have to try.

The next morning, Amy was drinking hot chocolate with Grandpa when Lou came down for breakfast alone.

"Hi," Amy greeted her sister, remembering the decision she had made the night before.

Lou smiled faintly.

"Did you have a good time last night?" Jack asked.

"Yes, thank you," Lou said, her voice subdued.

Jack looked closely at her. "Lou? Is there something the matter?"

"No," Lou replied. She sat down at the table and started fiddling with a pen, turning it around and around in her fingers. "Well, not *exactly*." She suddenly put the pen down and, taking a deep breath, looked at them both. "I guess you might as well know. Carl has been offered a new job in Chicago, and he's asked me to go with him."

Amy stared at her in astonishment. "But you're not going to, are you? Chicago's so far away!"

Lou didn't say anything.

"Lou?" Grandpa said.

"I've told him I'll think about it," Lou replied at last. "But I think — I think I might say yes."

# Chapter Six

Amy followed Lou up to the feed room. Despite all their arguments she really wanted Lou to stay at Heartland. They had spent so much of their lives apart, since Lou had decided to stay at her English boarding school when Amy and her mom had moved to Virginia to live with Grandpa. Amy felt that she was just starting to get to know her older sister, and she didn't want her to leave.

"You're not really going to go to Chicago, are you?" she asked. "What would you do there?"

"I'd get a job," Lou said, setting out the feed buckets. "I might even be able to transfer with my present company."

"But you'd go there just to be with Carl?" Amy questioned.

"Yes." Lou looked suddenly serious. "I would."

"It's so far away," Amy stammered. "Please don't go, Lou. Stay here with us."

Lou straightened up, her blue eyes angry. "What would be the point?" she snapped. "You've made it perfectly clear that you don't want my help around here."

Amy felt torn. She didn't like the changes that Lou kept suggesting for Heartland, but she desperately wanted her sister to stay. "I do. I —"

"Stop it, Amy!" Lou interrupted bitterly. "I know what you think. Don't try and pretend otherwise."

"But, Lou . . ."

"I don't want to talk about it!" Lou raised her voice. "And that's the end of the discussion!" Banging the buckets down on to the floor, she turned and walked out of the feed room.

❧

After breakfast, Carl and Lou got ready to leave for the airport. "Thank you for having me," Carl said, shaking hands with Grandpa. "It's been great." He turned to Amy and winked. "See you later."

"Bye," Amy said curtly. She wished he had never come. If it wasn't for him, Lou wouldn't be thinking about going away.

Lou tucked her arm through his. "Come on, we don't

want you to miss your plane." She turned to Grandpa. "I'll be back by lunchtime."

"Remember we're all going to the movies this afternoon," he reminded her.

Lou nodded.

"Wish I could stay," Carl said. "But work calls."

*Thank goodness!* Amy thought to herself.

After Carl and Lou had driven off, Amy went to Spartan's stall. She had decided to take him out to graze again.

Spartan's eyes rolled angrily, and he pawed the ground as she led him out of his stall. His ears were back, but Amy barely noticed. She couldn't stop thinking about Lou going to Chicago. Reaching the patch of grass, lost in her own world, she forgot she was leading Spartan and loosened her grip on the lead rope.

Moving like a striking snake, Spartan pulled backward, half rearing as he jerked his head up and out of her reach. The rope slipped through Amy's hands, burning her skin as it went. She staggered back in surprise. "Spartan!" she gasped.

The horse swung around beside her, his heavy shoulder colliding with her and knocking her off balance. Amy felt herself falling and reached out too late. Her head crashed against a wooden fence post. Then she slid to the ground and lay there, dazed.

In front of her, Spartan rose up on his hind legs, his dark eyes glistened, and he shrieked savagely as his front legs thrashed out. Amy looked up and saw his flailing hooves above her. She screamed and closed her eyes.

"Stop it!" Jack Bartlett's voice shouted. Amy's eyes flew open. Red in the face and out of breath, her grandfather was grasping the end of the lead rope, frantically trying to pull the horse away. Distracted, Spartan shook his head wildly and turned to face Jack. Amy scrambled to her feet and, ignoring the wave of dizziness that swept over her, she flung herself at Spartan's head.

Spartan plunged backward at the touch of her hands on his halter, but she held on desperately. "Steady!" she cried. At last Spartan came to a stop, and he stood snorting, his body trembling with rage as he stared at her.

"Amy!" Grandpa exclaimed. "Are you OK?"

Amy nodded, not taking her eyes off Spartan for a second. "I'll put him back in his stall," she said. Not waiting for permission, she led Spartan toward the barn. Her legs felt weak with shock.

Quickly she put him in his stall and slipped out just in time before his hooves crashed defiantly into the wooden door.

The next moment Grandpa was beside her, his arms wrapping tightly around her. "Amy!" he exclaimed. "I thought he was going to kill you. I really did."

In the warmth and safety of his arms, the adrenaline left her and Amy's knees gave way. Grandpa supported her and helped her to the house. Then he gently checked her head. "You'll have a lump there in the morning, but I think it should be OK." He took her hand, his blue eyes shadowed with fear and relief. "When I looked out of the window and saw him knock you over, I could hardly watch. It was like my worst nightmare had come true."

"Thank goodness you were watching," Amy said with a cold shiver running down her spine at the thought of what might have happened if Grandpa hadn't been there.

Jack Bartlett stroked her hair. "That horse is vicious, Amy. I know it's hard, but we're going to have to put him down."

Amy stared at him. "Grandpa! We can't do that to him."

"Amy," her grandpa started, his voice firmer than she had ever heard it, "a horse like Spartan will never be cured. I know it's hard to accept, but he's just one of those horses that Heartland can't help. We need to talk to Scott." Amy opened her mouth to argue. But Grandpa wouldn't let her speak. "I'm sorry, but I'm not going to change my mind." He squeezed her shoulder. "You are far more precious to me than any horse."

Amy's voice rose desperately. "But, Grandpa . . ."

"No, Amy," Grandpa said sadly. "No buts. Not this time." He sighed. "Now, I think you should go lie down and rest for a while."

Amy walked numbly up the stairs. Pulling off her jeans, she got into bed. She couldn't stand by and watch Spartan be put down. She had to give him one more chance.

Then it came to her. *Join up!* She hadn't tried it before because she had been worried about what Spartan would do — but this was her last chance. It was *his* last chance. By joining up with him she might be able to win back his trust. Hope rushed through her. Spartan might try to escape, but it was a risk she was prepared to take if there was a chance that his life might be saved.

She sat up in bed. When could she do it? It had to be a time when no one was around. Grandpa would never let her anywhere near Spartan again.

Just then, there was a knock on her bedroom door, and her grandpa came in. "How are you feeling?" he asked.

"My head hurts a bit still," Amy replied. "But I'm OK."

"Looks like we shouldn't go to the movies this afternoon," Grandpa said.

The movies! Amy had forgotten about going to the movies. A plan quickly formed in her mind. Putting a hand to her head, she lay back down. "Well, my head hurts too much to go, but you should go with Lou," she said. "You could still go. I'll be fine here."

Grandpa shook his head. "I can't leave you after a knock like that."

"I'll phone Matt. He'll come over," Amy said.

Grandpa didn't look convinced.

"It would be good for you and Lou to spend the time together," Amy said. "You could talk to her about going to Chicago. She'll probably open up more if I'm not there." Amy looked at Grandpa. "You don't want her to go, do you?"

"Of course I don't, but it's up to her." Grandpa seemed lost in thought for a moment.

"If you don't let her know how much we need her, she'll never stay," Amy pleaded.

"It would be good to have a chance to talk with her, find out what's she's thinking." Grandpa stood up. "We'll see how you're feeling in a couple of hours."

❧

By the afternoon, Amy had finally managed to convince Grandpa and Lou that she was quite happy to be left on her own. She'd given Matt a call. "I'll be fine," she said when Grandpa came to her room after lunch. "I called Matt," she said, but she didn't mention that Matt had been out playing basketball and that she'd told his mom that he didn't need to call back.

"OK," Grandpa said. "But we won't be long. Promise me you'll rest."

"I promise," Amy said.

Grandpa frowned. "Maybe we should wait for Matt to get here."

"No!" Amy said quickly. She saw his look of surprise. "If you don't leave now, you'll miss the movie."

"I guess you're right," Grandpa said reluctantly. He bent down and kissed her. "You take care."

Amy nodded and faked a yawn. "I think I'll go to sleep for a while."

Grandpa looked relieved. "Good girl. See you later."

Amy lay in her bed and listened to his footsteps going downstairs and then to the sounds of Grandpa and Lou getting into the car and the engine starting. Getting out of bed, she crept to the window and watched them driving off.

She waited a few minutes to make sure they were safely gone and then pulled on her jeans and ran down the stairs and out of the house. It was quiet in the yard. The air felt heavy and still and the horses were barely shifting in their stalls. In the distance, dark clouds were gathering. Amy felt sure a storm was brewing.

She fetched a longline from the tack room and then, with her heart thudding in her chest, she approached Spartan's stall. The quietness on the yard was so unusual that, for a moment, Amy felt a flicker of loneliness. She felt as though she was completely on her own. Alone with Spartan. She took a deep breath. It was the way it had to be.

She opened the stall door. Spartan leaped backward, his muscles gathered under his bay coat, his neck high. Adrenaline coursing through her, Amy slipped inside. "Easy, boy," she said.

Spartan snorted, the sound reverberating in the still air. Talking all the while, Amy approached him. The horse's hindquarters swung around, but Amy moved quickly, closing in on his head and taking hold of his halter before he could kick out. "Oh, Spartan," she said in desperation. "You don't need to be afraid of me."

Taking another deep breath, Amy clipped the longline to the halter and led him out. He pranced angrily beside her. A heavy drop of rain fell on Amy's arm and then another, but she ignored them. Rain or no rain, she only had this one chance with Spartan. In a couple of hours Grandpa and Lou would be back and her chance would be gone.

She led Spartan into the ring, securing the gate behind her. As she took him into the middle, she looked anxiously at the fence. It wasn't very high, just over four feet. He could probably clear it easily. Her fingers hesitated by the clip of the longline. What if he escaped? But what choice did she have? With one swift move she un-hooked the line. It was a risk she would just have to take. She stepped back.

Spartan jerked his head and stopped, a look of sur-prise on his face. Realizing that he was free, he let out a wild snort and tossed his head in the air, wheeling around on his back legs. Then to Amy's horror he set off straight toward the fence.

"Stop!" she shouted, running after him.

Spartan jerked to a halt, his front feet stamping into the sand. He spun around and looked at her. Amy stopped in her tracks. She was caught in the savage glare of his eyes. For the first time *ever* in her life she re-alized that she felt afraid of a horse. And she was sud-denly aware of how horribly vulnerable she was with only the longline in her hand. She took an uncertain step backward. There was a sudden roll of thunder, and with a screaming cry Spartan plunged toward her.

As he thundered over the sand, Amy's fear suddenly disappeared, drowned in the wave of blind fury that swept over her. How *dare* he attack her! After she had de-fended him, cared for him, believed in him! With every bit of strength in her body she flung the longline toward him. "*No!*" she shouted, almost incoherent with rage.

Startled by the flying rope, Spartan swerved and gal-loped past her. Amy grabbed the rope from the ground. "You can't blame me!" she screamed. "It wasn't my fault!" Stopping abruptly, Spartan turned and reared, his eyes gleaming with fury. His front legs flailed in the air. Amy slashed the rope toward him again. "It wasn't my fault!" she screamed, advancing on him. "It wasn't my fault!"

With a sudden snort of alarm Spartan came down and galloped away from her. There was a loud crash as a second clap of thunder burst overhead. The rain started to beat down with a new intensity, but Amy barely noticed it. Picking up the rope, she flung it after Spartan. "Go on!" she shouted. "Go on! Get away!"

Wherever he went she followed with the rope. White-hot anger coursed through her. Overhead a jagged fork of lightning blazed down through the sky. Water streamed down Amy's face, her tears mingling with the pouring rain. On and on Spartan galloped, his coat streaked with sweat and rain as she forced him on through the crashing of the storm.

She had no idea how long she drove him around the ring. But after many, many circles the rage seemed to start leaving Spartan's eyes. Amy saw his gallop steady and his inside ear flicker toward her. A shock ran through her. It was the *first signal* of a join up! Spartan's wild circles, his attempts to escape from her had led to the first stage of a join up. There was no mistaking it — his inside ear was fixed on her, his gallop was slowing to a steady canter.

Gasping for breath and soaked to the skin, she acted instinctively. She squared her shoulders with his and stepped slightly into his path. He picked up on the cue and turned. He started around in the opposite direction, his eyes fixed on her.

More circles. She hardly noticed that the thunder had passed. She wasn't satisfied yet. His acceptance of her had to be absolute. They had to have an understanding. And then it happened; he started to chew. Stretching his head down until his muzzle was almost on the ground, he trotted in circles, his mouth chewing at the air, his neck stretched long and low.

Amy took a step back and turned her body away, dropping her eyes to the ground. From the corner of her eye she could see Spartan stop. He looked at her. His ears pricked. There was a long pause. She blocked out the thought of what Spartan had done the last time she'd turned her back to him. She heard him take a step and chills ran down the back of her neck, but she forced herself to stay still, with her eyes looking down. The breath rasped in her throat, her heart pounded. What if he decided to attack her again? He was close now, getting closer. She could hear his hooves thudding softly into the wet sand, hear his heavy breathing.

Suddenly, she felt warm breath on the back of her neck, a muzzle on her shoulder. Hardly daring to breathe, she turned slowly around. Spartan stood there. His sides were heaving, his coat was streaked with rain and sweat, but the fire and fear had left his eyes. Very gently, Amy reached out and rubbed his face. For the first time since coming to Heartland, Spartan accepted her touch.

Amy felt her eyes filling with tears, and she suddenly realized it had stopped raining. Tears of relief and joy washed away the weeks of unrelenting guilt. "Spartan," she whispered. She caught the sob that rose in her throat. "It wasn't my fault," she whispered, leaning her head against his wet neck. "It really wasn't my fault."

As the tears on her face dripped onto Spartan's steaming neck, she suddenly knew that it was true — she wasn't to blame for the accident. As Grandpa had said, her mom would never have gone out that night if she hadn't wanted to. Fresh tears sprang to Amy's eyes, tears that welled from the very depth of her heart — tears of grief and loss, no longer held back by the crushing weight of guilt. Wrapping her arms around Spartan's neck, she sobbed into his mane and took comfort in their new understanding.

At long last her sobs softened and Spartan's breathing slowed. Amy drew back and realized that the clouds were parting. The sun was shining through, making the leaves on the trees surrounding the schooling ring shimmer and glow.

A new determination filled her, hot and fierce. She would never be able to bring her mom back, but she could help Spartan. She kissed him on the neck. "I promise I'll make you better, Spartan," she whispered as he turned and focused on her. "I promise." As she looked into his dark eyes, she knew that her mom would have approved. She knew her mom would have done the same thing.

Amy slowly led Spartan back to his stall where she fetched a hay net and rubbed him down. As she rubbed his back with the cloth she suddenly paused. Right by his withers he seemed to have a patch of white hairs coming through. It was the first time she had been close enough to see. She examined the area closely, parting the hair with her fingers. Her eyes widened. It was an old freeze mark. The fur over the freeze mark had been dyed brown to match his coat, but now the white hair was growing out. Amy thought that the people who had stolen him must have dyed the hair so Spartan couldn't be traced. Amy looked more closely. It was impossible to read the letters with the two colors of hair, but maybe if the area was clipped the letters would become more visible. Excitement surged through Amy. Maybe she could find Spartan's old owners. Maybe he could be reunited with them and lead a normal life again.

She finished rubbing him down and then sank into some straw by the feed bin. Spartan was pulling happily at the sweet-smelling hay. Amy watched him, marveling at the change in his eyes and demeanor. Relaxed and peaceful, he munched on his hay, occasionally swishing his tail.

*He could do with a good brushing*, Amy thought, but then she yawned, too exhausted to move. She could do it later. Leaning her head back, she closed her eyes. *Just two minutes' rest*, she thought. Her eyelashes flickered on her cheeks. Within seconds she was fast asleep.

# Chapter Seven

"Amy! Oh, my God!"

Amy woke up with a jump at the sound of Lou's voice. Confused, she blinked and looked up.

Lou was staring down at her, her face pale. "Grandpa! Quick!" she shouted over her shoulder. "Amy's collapsed in Spartan's stall!"

"No, I'm OK," Amy said hastily, scrambling to her feet. "I just fell asleep."

Jack Bartlett came hurrying up to the door. "What on earth are you doing in there?" he demanded.

Amy saw the fear on his face. "I'm OK," she repeated. She hastened to explain. "Spartan's better." She moved toward the horse.

"Amy! Come out of there at once," Lou said, her voice piercing.

"No. Look!" Amy put her hand gently on Spartan's shoulder, hoping he would respond positively — that the join up really had been a success. He turned his head to her inquiringly. Amy was relieved to see that his eyes were calm. She moved around to the front of him and rubbed his forehead. "See," she said, turning to Grandpa and Lou, who were watching, openmouthed.

"What's happened to him?" Lou gasped.

"I joined up with him, and now he trusts me." As she spoke, Amy realized how inadequate the words seemed. She could never fully convey the experience she remembered — the explosion of fury and guilt, the anger, the fear. All mirrored in the violent storm that had reminded her of the night of the accident. She had never experienced anything like it and, amazing as it had been, she hoped to never have to go through anything like it again.

Lou and Grandpa looked at her with disbelief, but the evidence was there for them to see. As Amy stroked him, Spartan stood, gentle as little Sugarfoot.

Grandpa opened the stall door. "Amy Fleming," he said, running a despairing hand through his hair, "I didn't want you ever to go near Spartan again."

"I know. I'm sorry," Amy said. She grinned at him. "But aren't you glad I did?" She came out of the stall. "You know Mom would have done the same thing, Grandpa."

Jack Bartlett looked at her for a moment and then

swept her into his arms. "Yes, honey," he said, kissing her hair. "I know she would."

✤

Amy called Scott to let him know about the break-through and about the freeze mark she had found on Spartan's back. And then for the first time in a long time, she slept peacefully through the night.

Amy got up early the next morning. The sun was shining in through her window. Pulling on her clothes, she went outside.

The trees on the ridges of the hills that rose behind Heartland stood out dark green against the pale blue of the sky. She looked around, breathing in deeply, enjoying the cool of the morning air. She felt wonderfully refreshed and determined in her resolve to do everything she could to help Spartan.

As soon as Ty arrived she filled him in on the events of the day before and took him to see Spartan.

"I thought if we clipped the hair, the freeze mark might show up more clearly," she said.

"I'll get the clippers," Ty agreed. When he came back Spartan was nuzzling at Amy's shoulder. He shook his head. "I'm going to take days off more often!" he joked. "He's a different horse."

Amy patted Spartan. "He's not. He's just back to being the horse he was."

"Thanks to you," Ty said. "You believed in him, Amy. He wouldn't have had a chance without you."

Amy felt her cheeks turn pink.

Spartan moved beside them. "Well . . . I guess we'd better get this clipping done," Ty said, his voice suddenly brisk.

Amy moved to the side of Spartan's head. "Easy now," she murmured to the horse as Ty switched the clippers on. Spartan flinched but settled down as Amy stroked him.

It only took a minute. "All done," Ty said, turning the clippers off.

Amy looked eagerly at the rectangle of clipped hair. Six white numbers stood out clearly against Spartan's bay coat.

Ty pulled a pen and a piece of paper out of his pocket. He scribbled down the numbers. "Now all we need to do is call and ask Scott to have the number traced."

"I wonder what Spartan's owners are like," Amy said.

"I guess we'll find out," Ty said.

Amy took the piece of paper with the number on it and went down to the house to use the phone in the kitchen. She called Scott, and he explained how he'd make some calls to try to trace Spartan's owner. "Although," he warned her, "sometimes they don't have up-to-date information. I'll see what I can find out."

As Amy put the phone down she realized Lou had overheard the conversation.

"I hope he can find them," Lou said. "Especially now that you've cured him."

"Well, *started* curing him," Amy corrected her. She knew that Spartan wasn't completely better yet. He needed to build up his confidence with everyone. She was about to end the conversation and then hesitated. All their disagreements suddenly seemed so pointless. "So what are you up to?"

"Just running through the list of things that I still have to organize for this dance," Lou replied.

"Is there anything I can do to help?" Amy asked.

Lou looked up, her blue eyes showing her surprise. "But you think the whole thing's a stupid idea," she said. "Why would you want to help?"

Amy's cheeks flushed. "I don't think it's stupid. Well, maybe I did at first," she admitted, seeing Lou's expression. "But people want to come, and I . . . I hope it works." She smiled at Lou, suddenly realizing how much she meant it.

❧

After Amy did her chores and worked with Raisin for a while, she devoted the next couple of hours to bonding further with Spartan. She took him out in the circular ring and joined up with him again and then spent an hour grooming him, trying to brush out the dirt and grease that had built up in his coat over the past few weeks. Finally, she massaged diluted lavender oil around his nostrils to help soothe and relax him.

Ty looked over the door as she was finishing. "Lavender," he said, sniffing the air. "That's a good idea."

Amy nodded. "Can you think of anything else that might be helpful? He's been through so much, I want to help him feel really comfortable."

"How about some walnut-flower remedy?" Ty said. "Your mom used to use it on horses that were getting used to new situations. You could also give him a tablespoon of honey in his feed."

"Yeah," Amy said, pleased with the idea. She knew that honey was excellent for channeling energy. Her mom had said that it sometimes made difficult horses more manageable. It energized them and also made them willing to please.

Just then there was the sound of a car coming up the drive. "It's Matt and Scott," Ty said.

Amy came out of the stall.

"Hi!" she called as the Jeep came to a halt and Matt and Scott jumped out.

"Hi, Amy," Scott called. "Hi, Ty."

"Hey, guys," Ty said.

"That's great news about Spartan!" Matt said to Amy as they reached the stall. "Scott told me. You must be really happy."

"Spartan's like a different horse," Ty said. "You should see how he is with Amy."

Scott watched as Amy went into the stall and patted Spartan. She even picked his hooves. "You've had a real breakthrough," he said. "Well done!"

Amy's eyes sparkled as she came over to the door. "It was all because I joined up with him. I probably should have tried it sooner."

"Have you heard any news from the freeze-mark agency or from Spartan's owner?" Amy asked.

"Not yet," Scott replied. "If they make a match, they'll contact the owner."

"Bet you can't wait to hear," Matt said. "Then Spartan can go back to his real home."

"I guess," Amy said. She tried to sound more positive. "Yeah. It will be good."

"But it will be hard to say good-bye after all this, huh?" Scott said, looking sympathetically at her.

Amy nodded and caught Ty's eye. "Very."

"So you *don't* want him to go?" Matt said, sounding confused. "But I thought you wanted his owners to get in touch."

"I did — I do," Amy said. She saw the confusion on Matt's face. It was obvious he didn't understand. She sighed, wishing, not for the first time, that Matt understood her feelings about horses in the way Scott and Ty did. Maybe then, imagining him as a boyfriend wouldn't be so hard.

❧

After lunch, as Amy came out of the house, she heard a low whinny. She looked at the front stable block, expecting to see Pegasus's head over his stall door, but it wasn't Pegasus, it was Spartan. He whickered again. Amy smiled. "Hi there, boy." She walked over and stroked his face.

As she played with the whiskers on his lower lip, she thought about how she was going to rehabilitate him. Amy knew it wasn't enough for him simply to trust her — he had to learn to have confidence in other people as well. She would have to get as many people as possible to handle him — Grandpa, Lou, Ty, and Scott when he came by.

She smoothed his long forelock. And what about riding him? A thrill ran through her at the thought. When should she try that? She decided to ask Ty what he thought.

She found him filling the evening hay nets from the small stock of hay in the feed room. "Hi," he said, looking up as she came in.

"I was thinking," Amy blurted out her question, "when do you think I should try riding Spartan?" She felt the breath catch in her throat, anticipating Ty's answer. She respected his opinion and knew that as much as she wanted to ride Spartan, if Ty told her to wait a month then she would.

Ty shrugged. "The end of the week?" he suggested.

"That soon?" Amy said.

"Sure." Ty nodded. "If he continues to improve, then why put it off? It should help his confidence. You'll be able to take him out and see how he deals with new experiences."

Excitement flooded through Amy. The end of the week! She couldn't wait!

❧

Over the next few days, Amy spent as much time as she could with Spartan, handling him, grooming him, lunging him, and getting other people to come into his stall and handle him, too. Gradually, the lingering nervousness started to leave his eyes. However, a certain reserve seemed to remain. Amy was puzzled by it. Spartan was affectionate and his confidence seemed to grow every day, but it was as if he was holding something back. Wondering whether she was imagining it all, she didn't mention it to anyone, and no one else — not even Ty — seemed to notice.

On Friday morning, she was grooming Spartan when

Ty looked over the door. "Thought any more about riding him?" he asked.

"Yeah, like always," Amy said. "I can't wait."

"So why not today?" Ty said.

"Today?" Amy said, her heart leaping with excitement. "You think he's ready?"

"Yeah," Ty replied. "Do you want me to get a saddle and bridle?"

Amy nodded eagerly. Her fingers trembled with anticipation as she quickly finished grooming Spartan. Thoughts whirled through her brain. She was going to get to ride Spartan! What would he be like? He looked fantastic to ride. Her heart raced as she remembered that she knew nothing about him before the accident. He might not even have been ridden before. He might throw her off. She ran her fingers through Spartan's mane and kissed his neck. She didn't care. She just wanted to try.

When Ty returned with the tack, Spartan sniffed at the bridle curiously but didn't seem to object when Amy took it and slipped it on over his head.

"Now for the saddle," she said, trying to keep her voice calm, although her stomach was fluttering nervously. Spartan's reaction to the saddle would give them a good indication if he had been ridden before. But he stood still as she placed the saddle and pad on his back and tightened the girth.

"So far, so good," Ty said, glancing at her. "He wouldn't be this calm if he hadn't been ridden before."

Amy nodded in relief. "Now, I've just got to get on."

"I'd lunge him first," Ty said. "Just to get him used to moving with the saddle and bridle on and give him a chance to get rid of some energy."

They led Spartan up to the training ring, and Amy started to lunge him. He bucked once as he first moved into a trot but then settled into a steady rhythm. After five minutes Amy brought him to a halt and looked at Ty.

"Here goes," she said, pulling the stirrups down.

Ty moved to Spartan's head and held the reins while Amy mounted. She felt Spartan move nervously as she sank lightly down into the saddle, but she patted his neck and soothed him until he settled.

Amy picked up his reins and gently squeezed with her legs. Spartan walked forward. He felt calm and relaxed, and after a few laps around the ring, Amy started to relax, too. She shortened her reins and squeezed him into a trot. With his long stride he seemed to float across the sand.

"He's perfect!" she said as she passed Ty.

After a while, Amy asked Spartan to canter, and he made the transition smoothly. She cantered three circles, grinning with delight. Riding Spartan was just as fantastic as she had imagined.

At last she drew him to a halt. "Wow!" she gasped,

patting his warm bay neck and smiling at Ty in delight. "He's the best!"

"He looked great," Ty said.

Amy took her feet out of the stirrups and dismounted. "I'd better make that do for today," she said.

"Something tells me you'll be riding him again tomorrow," Ty said with a grin.

"I think you might be right." She smiled back.

Ty opened the gate, and Amy led Spartan down the yard. Just as she finished cooling him, the phone rang. Leaving the tack outside the stall, Amy ran to the house. She reached the phone just before Lou, who had come in from collecting vegetables from the back garden.

"Heartland," Amy said breathlessly. "Amy Fleming speaking."

"Hi." The man's voice was deep. "My name's Larry Boswell. I've been contacted by the freeze-mark agency. I believe you are boarding a horse of mine — a bay with a white star. He was stolen a few months ago."

It was Spartan's owner!

"Hello . . . are you there?" the man said.

"Yes — yes, I am," Amy said quickly.

"And do you have my horse?" the man inquired.

"Yes," Amy said, her stomach seeming to flip over. "We do."

# Chapter Eight

"That's fantastic news!" Larry Boswell said. "I can't believe you found him!" Amy could hear the emotion in his voice. "I never thought I'd see him again. He was stolen just over two months ago. How long have you had him?"

"Almost two weeks," Amy said. "But he was at the local vet's for six weeks before that."

"The vet's?"

Amy explained about the accident, and Larry Boswell listened intently. When she had finished, he whistled. "That's awful. I'm really sorry to hear about your mom. I can't thank you enough for taking Gerry in after all you've been through."

"Gerry?" Amy echoed.

"That's his name. Short for Geronimo. Full name Dancing Grass Geronimo," Larry Boswell told her. "He's one of my best stallions. I have a stud farm — I breed Morgans. Now, when would it be suitable for me to come over and pick him up? My farm's about two hours away."

*Pick him up.* Amy's mouth felt suddenly dry. "Well . . . er . . . whenever you like," she stammered. After all she had been through with Spartan the thought of losing him was hard to grasp. *But you wanted to find his owners,* she reminded herself. *You wanted Spartan to be happy.*

"Great!" said Larry Boswell. "I'll be over this after-noon, about three o'clock. Can you give me some direc-tions?"

By the time she put the phone down, Amy was feeling stunned. For a moment she was unable to move.

"What's wrong?" Lou asked.

"Spartan's owner is coming to collect him today."

"But that's great!" Lou exclaimed. She saw Amy's face and frowned uncertainly. "Isn't it?"

Tears prickled at the back of Amy's eyes. She nodded.

"You're going to miss him, aren't you?" Lou said softly.

Amy swallowed.

Lou put her arm around her. "It's the right thing, Amy. He couldn't stay here. At least this way he'll go to people he knows and who love him."

Amy knew she was right. Horses came to Heartland to be healed so they could then go to new homes or back to their owners. It was a rule their mom had insisted upon and Amy had grown up with. But somehow with Spartan it was different.

"I don't want him to go," she whispered.

"I know you don't," Lou said, hugging her. "But it's for the best. You know it is. We can't keep him here if he has the chance of a happy life with someone else."

Amy fought back her tears and nodded reluctantly.

From two thirty on, Amy waited in the kitchen with Lou and Ty, watching the drive.

"What did he sound like?" Ty asked Amy.

"OK, I guess," she replied, pacing back and forth.

"It'll be fine," Lou said. "You'll see. Stop worrying." She looked down the drive. "Here's Scott."

Amy had been in touch with the vet soon after speaking to Larry Boswell to tell him the news.

Scott parked his Cherokee and came into the house. "Not here yet?"

Amy shook her head.

Ten minutes later, a pickup pulling a trailer came up the drive. "It's him!" Amy exclaimed, her stomach turning with anticipation.

The pickup stopped. A short, husky man with gray hair got out. "Hi," he said, as they came out of the farmhouse to meet him. "I'm Larry Boswell."

Lou took charge of the situation and introduced everyone. Larry shook hands. "I can't tell you how pleased I am." He looked at Amy. "Like I said on the phone, I own a stud farm — but Gerry, he's always been real special to me. "I hand-reared him as a foal." His eyes scanned the stalls eagerly. "Where is he?"

Amy swallowed. "I'll get him," she said.

Spartan was in his stall. As Amy entered, he pricked his ears and nickered a welcome. Amy thought he looked beautiful. He still had some scars — they would stay with him forever — but his bay coat gleamed, his tail hung below his hocks, soft and silky, and the star on his forehead stood out, snowy white. "Oh, Spartan," she whispered, her heart aching. "It's time to say good-bye."

As she untied the rope he nuzzled affectionately against her. Giving him a kiss, Amy led him out of the stall.

Larry Boswell was looking around eagerly. "Gerry!" he exclaimed as soon as he saw him.

Spartan stopped dead at the sound of Larry Boswell's voice. His head flew up. His ears pricked. A shrill whinny burst from him, and he plunged in the direction of Larry, pulling the lead rope right out of Amy's hands. The horse trotted over and stopped in front of his owner.

"Hey, Gerry, Gerry boy," Larry Boswell murmured, stroking the horse's ears and neck and face. "I never thought I'd see you again."

Amy stood, astonished, rooted to the spot where

Spartan had left her. She watched as the horse nuzzled Larry Boswell ecstatically. There was no mistaking the connection between the two.

Larry Boswell gently examined the scars along Spartan's side. "You're not going to be winning much in the showring from now on, are you, buddy?" he said ruefully, but then he patted the horse. "We'll have to leave winning those ribbons to your foals."

"Foals?" Amy said, eagerly stepping forward. "He's got foals?"

"Not yet," Larry Boswell said. "I'd just used him for conformation classes until he was stolen. But I'll put him to stud when I get him home. He should breed some good stock."

Amy's eyes widened. Larry Boswell obviously hadn't realized that Spartan had been gelded. "Um . . ." she said, glancing quickly at Scott for support. "You won't be able to use him for breeding."

Larry frowned. "Why not?"

Scott stepped forward. "He's been gelded, I'm afraid."

"What?" Larry replied in genuine astonishment.

Scott nodded. "It's the policy here at Heartland. Until last week there was no way of seeing his freeze mark or even knowing for sure that he had been stolen. It was assumed that he would be rehomed, so he had to be gelded."

"What!" Mr. Boswell exclaimed incredulously. "This horse is," he corrected himself, "*was* a valuable breeding animal." He glared at Amy. "How could you do this? He was my most valuable stallion."

"We had no idea," Amy stammered, taken aback by his sudden anger.

Larry Boswell's voice rose. "He's got some of the best bloodlines in my stock. His foals would have brought thousands of dollars!"

"I'm sorry," Amy said, feeling close to tears. "I really am, I —"

"You'll be hearing from my lawyers about this!" Larry shouted.

Lou stepped forward. "Now, Mr. Boswell, please . . ."

But he ignored her. Letting go of Spartan, he pushed past Amy and Lou and headed toward his car. Ty grabbed Spartan, who had tried to follow him.

"Mr. Boswell —" Lou cried. "What about your horse?"

"This horse here doesn't resemble any horse that I know!" Larry Boswell shouted.

Scott stepped out in front of the angry man. "I think you should consider carefully what you are saying, Mr. Boswell," he said, his voice calm but full of authority. Mr. Boswell pulled up short. There was no way he could push Scott's tall, broad-shouldered frame out of the way. "Amy and her family took in your horse," Scott continued, looking around at Amy and Lou. "Despite their own tragic loss, they looked after him, made every effort to trace you. In my opinion you should be thanking them, not threatening them with legal action."

"Yes — but —" Larry blustered, his face flushing a deep red.

"Thanks to them you still have a horse," Scott said firmly. "Believe me, Mr. Boswell, you have *every* reason to be grateful."

For a moment, Larry looked as if he was going to argue further, but then his shoulders suddenly seemed to sag. "You're right," he muttered.

Amy felt the breath leave her in a rush. She met Lou's eyes and saw her relief.

Larry shook his head. "I guess you did what you had to, and I appreciate all the heartbreak that you've been through on his behalf." He glanced at Spartan. "But Gerry being gelded changes everything."

Amy was astonished. "Why?"

Larry Boswell shrugged. "What use would he be? I have a business to run. I can't have a horse that won't pay it's way."

Amy couldn't believe what she was hearing. "But you can't just leave him here!" she exclaimed.

"Well, I'm not going to take him back with me," Larry said. "I'll pay your expenses for keeping him until you find him a new home. But that's the best I can offer."

Amy looked at Spartan who was now shaking his

head, trying to pull away from Ty. Spartan loved his owner — that was completely clear. Although she didn't want to have to say good-bye to him, she knew that he belonged with Larry Boswell.

She stepped toward him. "Take Spartan with you," she pleaded.

But Larry Boswell shook his head. "Sorry, young lady. That's the way it has to be." He walked slowly toward Spartan. "You know the rules, Gerry," he said softly. "I can't break them, not even for you." He reached up and gently stroked the horse's forehead. "No, not even for you." He turned to Amy. "I'll send you the ownership papers," he said. "Bill me for the boarding fees." Squaring his shoulders, he strode back to his car.

As Larry drove away, Spartan let out a high-pitched whinny and pulled forward. "Easy boy," Ty said hastily.

Amy looked at the distress on Spartan's face and had to fight back the tears welling in her eyes. She couldn't suppress a feeling of dislike for Larry Boswell. How could he do this to Spartan?

"Don't worry," Lou said calmly, her expression full of sympathy. "We'll find another home for him. You'll see."

"But he wants to be with his owner!" Amy cried.

"No, Lou's right, Amy," Scott said quickly. "There'll be other people who will want to give him a home. He's a fine horse."

Ty nodded in agreement and clicked his tongue. "Come on, fella, let's put you back in your stall."

As they followed Spartan to the barn, Lou looked gratefully at Scott. "Thanks for standing up to Mr. Boswell for us. I don't know what we'd have done if he had gone ahead and sued."

"He wouldn't have gotten anywhere," Scott said.

"Thanks anyway," Lou said. She patted Spartan's back as he went into his stall. "I'm just glad he's getting better." She turned to Scott. "I wanted to ask you about Sugarfoot. Would it be OK to put him out to graze in the field now? I've been cutting him fresh grass each day, but it's not really the same."

"Turning him out for a few hours each day should be fine," Scott said. "As long as the weather's good, of course. I'll just give him a quick checkup."

Scott grabbed his bag from the car and then went to Sugarfoot's stall with Amy and Lou. Sugarfoot was happily nibbling on the remains of grass that Lou had cut for him at lunchtime.

"How are you doing, boy?" Scott said to him, patting the Shetland's neck. He listened to Sugarfoot's heart and checked his breathing. "He's making fine progress," he said to Lou.

"Do you hear that, Sugarfoot? You're ready to go out in the paddock," Lou said. She turned to Amy. "Should we turn him out now? It's such a nice day."

"That would be great," Amy said, her heart lifting a little.

Lou put Sugarfoot's halter on and then led the Shetland out to the pasture just behind the back barn. The grass was lush, rich with clover, and dotted randomly with bright yellow buttercups. Sugarfoot's small ears pricked eagerly.

Amy opened the gate. The little pony trotted into the field, and putting his head down, he snorted.

"Look at him!" Lou said.

Suddenly, Sugarfoot sank down to his knees and rolled, sending two white butterflies fluttering up into the air. He jumped to his feet, shook, and then plunged his head down into the sweet grass and started to graze.

Lou smiled. "Isn't it incredible to see him like this?"

Amy nodded. She could vividly remember the shock of seeing Sugarfoot only a couple of weeks ago. Then he had been lying in his stall, breathing faintly, too weak to stand, half starved but too unhappy to eat. Now, here he was, grazing in the field. "It's so wonderful to see him happy again," she said.

"I know," said Lou, her eyes glowing. "I can't believe the change in him. There's nothing like seeing a sick animal recover. It's just such a good feeling!"

"I second that," Scott said softly.

"Better than clinching a deal at the bank?" Amy teased her as they started walking back to the house.

"Yes!" Lou said. "A million times better!"

Amy was surprised to see a black convertible Saab parked outside the farmhouse. The driver's door swung open as they approached.

"Carl!" Lou gasped. "What are you doing here?"

# Chapter Nine

❧

Carl stepped out of the car. "Well, that's a nice greeting," he said with a laugh.

Lou hurried forward. "You weren't supposed to be coming until tomorrow!"

"I took the day off." Carl put his arms around her. "I couldn't bear to be away from you another minute."

Lou pulled back. "Carl, this is Scott Trewin," she said, looking from one to the other, "our local vet. Scott, this is Carl Anderson."

Carl offered his hand to Scott. "Pleased to meet you."

Scott shook his hand. "Likewise," he said, but Amy noticed that his voice was cool. He turned to her. "I better go."

"Sure. Thanks for coming," she replied.

"Bye, Scott! Thanks again," Lou called after him.

Scott drove off in a cloud of exhaust fumes with the doors of his Cherokee rattling as usual.

Carl raised his eyebrows. "I would have thought a vet could afford an upgrade on that old Jeep model."

Before Amy could say anything, Lou leaped to Scott's defense. "Come on, Carl. Scott's a brilliant vet!" she said sharply. "Who cares if he doesn't have the newest Range Rover?"

Amy looked at her sister in surprise. It wasn't like Lou to sound so intense. Even though Lou had said it with a smile, she could tell her sister was serious.

As they went into the house, Lou started to tell Carl about Sugarfoot. "He's so much better," she said. "We just turned him out in the paddock, and it was so wonderful, he looked so happy!"

"Great," Carl said, sounding rather bored. He dumped his bag on the floor. "Any chance of a drink?"

Amy saw Lou's face fall in disappointment. He wasn't showing any interest in what she was saying to him. "Yeah, sure," Lou said flatly, and headed for the refrigerator.

❧

Leaving Lou and Carl in the house, Amy went back outside. She was sweeping the yard in front of the stable block and thinking about what they could do to find Spartan a home when Lou and Carl came out. The horses were all looking out over their stall doors. Lou walked over to Spartan and offered him a mint. But the bay horse ignored her as he stared down the drive, his ears pricked, his head up.

Lou stroked his neck. "Poor thing," she murmured. "Don't worry, we'll find you another home soon."

"You really think so?" Carl said. He scowled. "With those scars?"

Amy stopped brushing and glared at him. "Some people care about more than appearance!" she replied.

Carl frowned in genuine astonishment. "You mean there are actually people who wouldn't mind?"

"Of course there are!" Amy said hotly.

Lou stepped in hastily. "I guess the most important thing is that we find him the *right* home." She turned and began to walk along the row of horses, feeding them mints.

Carl followed her. "So how about Chicago?" he said, putting his arm around her. "Have you decided yet?"

Amy looked up. To her relief she saw that Lou was shaking her head. "No, not yet."

"I don't understand what the holdup is," Carl said.

"It's a big decision to make, Carl," Lou replied. "If I go to Chicago, I'll be leaving everything here."

"Oh, come on, Lou," Carl said. "You can't seriously want to go on playing country girl forever."

"Why not?" Lou said rather crossly.

"You love the city — you're great there," Carl replied.

"Don't try to tell me what I am!" Lou said.

Carl immediately backed off. "I'm sorry."

"Good," Lou said sharply. "Because I'm not going to be forced into anything. Going to Chicago is a decision I have to make on my own."

"I understand," Carl said. "You know I do, and I'd never interfere. I respect you far too much for that."

Lou looked slightly reassured and didn't seem to object when Carl slipped his arm around her shoulder again. "It's only because I want you to be with me so much," he said in a soft voice.

Amy didn't want to hear any more. She headed toward the paddock to get Sundance for a ride.

❧

The next morning, Amy decided to ride Spartan again. He was just as good in the training ring as he had been the day before, so she decided to take him out on the trails behind the pasture.

Spartan jogged excitedly as they rode along the path behind Heartland and up the hillside. It was a warm day, and Amy chose a shady trail. The sun slanted down between the canopy of leaves, casting shadows on the sandy ground. Spartan pricked his ears as he stepped among the trees. Amy could feel him start to tense up. She patted him and he flinched. "What's the matter?" she said. "It's OK."

Spartan walked cautiously on, his nostrils blowing, his neck outstretched. As they rounded the corner the trees thickened, blocking out the sun overhead. Spartan stopped and stared. Amy felt her stomach turn as she saw the canopy of trees. The sight of the path covered by the lush limbs of the trees brought a tidal wave of emotion over her as memories of the night of the accident flooded back.

Spartan sensed her fear and stepped backward, his hoof landing on a dry branch that broke with a resounding crack. With a terrified snort, Spartan reared high into the air.

"Spartan!" Amy gasped, throwing herself forward just in time. Spartan's front legs thrashed out, his eyes wide with fear. He landed on all four feet but in an instant was up in the air again, higher this time, so high he seemed on the point of crashing over backward. Losing her stirrup, Amy let go of the reins and hung on to Spartan's mane. He stayed balanced there for what seemed to Amy like an eternity and then came down and set off at a wild gallop along the path.

Amy clutched his mane desperately, grabbing for the reins, trying to get her stirrup back. "Spartan! Whoa!" she cried. But by now the horse was in a blind panic. He swerved around a corner and into a clearing.

Amy lurched in the saddle, but the tight turn simultaneously swung the reins toward her. She grabbed them and threw her weight backward, pulling hard. "Steady! Steady, boy!"

Spartan came to a halt, his sides heaving and his neck damp with sweat. Amy petted him. Her hands were trembling. What had she just done? In one unthinking moment, had she just wrecked all her good work with Spartan? She glanced back at the tunnel of trees. Suddenly, she was gripped with Spartan's fear. She wanted to get away, as far away as possible, from the memory of that awful night.

*Be calm.* Amy suddenly heard her mom's voice clear in her mind. *To be the horse's strength,* the voice whispered, *you must control your own fear.*

Amy took a deep breath. Her hands stopped shaking.

"You're all right, boy," she said to Spartan, her voice steady apart from a slight tremor. "What was all that about?"

Spartan's ears flickered. It took immense resolve, but Amy knew what she had to do. She shortened her reins and turned him back toward the trees. "Don't be scared," she said. "Nothing's going to happen to you."

She knew that Spartan couldn't understand her words, but she hoped that the tone of her voice would reassure him. She also knew that she had to get him back through the tunnel of trees or else his fear would grow and grow. "Walk on," she commanded.

Spartan hesitated.

"Walk on!" Amy said more firmly, nudging him with her heel.

This time Spartan did as she directed. He took a step forward and then another. Forcing down her own fear, Amy patted his neck as he walked cautiously through the canopy of trees. "Good boy!" she praised, patting him.

At last they were out on the other side. It was then and only then that Amy allowed herself to dismount. She leaned against Spartan, her legs feeling weak with relief. She had done it — they had made it through. He nuzzled her, his eyes calm again.

"Oh, Spartan," she said, patting him. He put his head down to graze. Amy sighed. No matter how much he had come along, there was such a long way to go before he would be ready to be rehomed. And then they had to find someone who would fully understand him.

She picked up the reins. "Come on, boy," she said, shaking her head. "Let's go home."

As she rode into the yard, Ty was coming out of Pegasus's stall. "How was he?" he asked.

"Not so good," Amy replied. She was about to explain what had happened when the kitchen door opened and Lou came hurrying out.

"Amy!" She looked very excited. "I'm so glad you're back!"

"Why? What's the matter?" Amy said.

"The most amazing thing has just happened!" Lou said. "I've just had a call from a father looking for a horse for his thirteen-year-old daughter. She sounds absolutely ideal!"

"Ideal for what?" Amy said in confusion.

Lou's eyes glowed. "For *Spartan*, of course! They read about us in a magazine and were delighted when I said we had a horse ready for rehoming!"

Amy stared at Lou. "You're not serious?"

"But they sound perfect." Lou looked at her in confusion. "I thought you'd be pleased. I thought you wanted to find Spartan a good home, and you said he's wonderful to ride."

"Not yet!" Amy exclaimed. "He's nowhere near ready. He still needs to build his trust in me and other people. You'll just have to call them back and tell them that he's not available."

"But they'll have already left. I told them they could come and see him right away. I thought it would be fine. They're even bringing their trailer."

"Lou!" Amy said incredulously. "How could you? Why didn't you check with me first?"

Lou looked like she didn't know what to say. "I'm — I'm sorry," she stammered. "But you weren't here — I thought you'd be pleased."

"That's great!" Amy said. "Just great!" She shook

her head. "Well, they can't have him. *You* can tell them that when they arrive!" Grabbing Spartan's reins, she marched into his stall.

"Amy! Wait!" Ty said, following her.

"What?" Amy said.

"Maybe it's not as bad as it sounds. Maybe they'd be willing to wait until he's ready. You should at least talk to them."

Amy frowned at him. "You mean, you think I should let them see Spartan?"

"Yeah. Why not?" Ty said.

Spartan nuzzled Amy's hand. She patted him. "But he needs a really special home," she said quietly.

"You're right — but maybe this is the one," Ty said.

Amy had a gut feeling that it wouldn't be, but she gave in. "OK," she said. "I guess they can have a look at him."

✧

The more Amy heard about the Satchwells from Lou, the more her reservations grew.

"Mr. Satchwell said that Melanie, his daughter, has been riding for three years," Lou explained as they waited for them to arrive after lunch. "She's just outgrown her old pony, and they want a horse that she can take to the local shows."

"They sound ideal," said Carl, who was waiting with them.

"They don't sound very experienced," Amy objected. "Where would they keep him?"

"At their boarding stable and riding school."

"But that would be all wrong for Spartan!" Amy exclaimed. "He needs a quiet home."

"Amy, it's OK — just give them a chance," Ty said in a reassuring voice.

Just then, a gleaming white BMW pulling a top-of-the-line trailer came slowly up the drive. The Satchwells got out.

"Max Satchwell," the father said, striding over toward Lou with his hand outstretched. "Pleased to meet you."

Lou introduced herself, Amy, Carl, and Ty.

"I'm Nancy," said Mrs. Satchwell, stepping gingerly over the gravel in her red open-toed sandals. "And this is Melanie, our daughter."

Amy looked Melanie Satchwell up and down. She was a couple of years younger than Amy, dressed in spotless breeches and tall black riding boots. She had red hair with tight curls. "Hi," she said brightly to Amy. "I read about you in a magazine. My friends couldn't believe it when I said I was coming here! They were *so* jealous!"

"Ever since she saw the article, Melanie's been wanting a horse from here," Max Satchwell said, smiling fondly at his daughter. "Haven't you, pumpkin?"

Melanie ignored her father and looked around impatiently. "Can I see the horse?" she said eagerly.

"He's over there," Amy said, pointing to where Spartan was looking out over his stall door.

"The bay with the star?" Melanie said. Amy nodded. "Wow! He's gorgeous!" Before Amy could stop her, Melanie had started running toward Spartan's door. Spartan snorted in alarm and shot backward into his stall. "He doesn't seem very friendly," Melanie exclaimed, stopping dead and looking surprised.

"It's because you were running!" Amy tried to explain. "He's a rescue horse. He's nervous. You need to be careful."

Melanie looked embarrassed. "I'm sorry. Piper doesn't mind me running. He isn't nervous about anything."

"Well, Spartan is," Amy said, a little too sharply. "He's been through a lot."

Melanie looked over the door. "He's got a lot of scars," she said. For a moment Amy wondered if it would stop her wanting him, but her hopes were dashed — Melanie turned around with a determined look on her face. "I want him, Daddy."

Max Satchwell reached in his pocket and got out his checkbook. He grinned at Lou. "Melanie always knows what she wants," he said. "Lucky we brought the trailer with us, eh? Now, you told me that you ask for a donation to Heartland. What sort of figure are we talking about?"

Amy couldn't stand it any longer. If Lou wouldn't say

anything, then she would. "You can't have him today!" she burst out. "He isn't ready yet . . ."

Max interrupted her. "Not ready?" He looked swiftly at Lou. "But you told me on the telephone that this horse needed a new home."

Lou flushed. "I'm sorry — it seems I spoke too soon."

Carl cut in smoothly. "It was a slight misunderstanding. However, if your daughter likes the horse, a deposit will secure him for her, Mr. Satchwell."

Amy stared at him in outrage. How *dare* he say that a deposit would secure Spartan! She swung around to Lou only to find that Lou was looking just as angry.

"A deposit will not secure him," Lou said in a controlled voice. "Spartan will only go when we are sure he's cured and that we've found him the right home." She turned to Mr. Satchwell and to Amy's astonishment apologized. "I am sorry, truly I am, that I didn't explain things fully on the telephone. But we have a policy of selecting new homes for our horses very, very carefully. People cannot just come and choose a horse, particularly a horse like Spartan who has been so badly traumatized. He needs a home with an experienced rider."

Max Satchwell looked outraged. "You mean you're not going to let my daughter have this horse?"

Lou shook her head. "No, I'm afraid not." She smiled quickly at Amy and then turned to Melanie, her eyes sympathetic. "Please try to understand, Melanie. We don't mean to be unfair. It's just that I don't think Spartan would be the right horse for you. We do have other horses you might be interested in though. There's — "

"You've already wasted enough of my time, Ms. Fleming," Max interrupted. "We'll be leaving right away!"

"Hold on, Daddy!" Melanie exclaimed suddenly. "I want to see the other horses."

The Satchwells and Amy looked at her in amazement. Amy had been sure that she would stalk off when she was told that she couldn't have Spartan, but it seemed she had been wrong about Melanie.

Melanie walked over to her father. "They're right, Daddy," she said calmly. "I probably don't want a horse that I have to be real careful around all the time. But maybe they have another horse that isn't so nervous."

"We have several actually," Lou said, looking as if she couldn't believe her ears. "Don't we, Amy?"

Amy nodded. "Do you want to come with me and have a look around?" she asked Melanie. "You might like Copper — he's not at all nervous, and he needs a good home with lots of activity."

"Can I see him?" Melanie asked eagerly.

"Sure," Amy replied. "Come on." She set off with Melanie toward the barn. As they walked, Amy told Melanie about Copper's history and told her that he had been abused, so she would need to be gentle with him, expecially around his head.

An hour later, Melanie had completely fallen in love with Copper. Melanie had been very sweet when she tacked up Copper, and as Amy watched the younger girl ride him around the schooling ring, she smiled. Copper was a young horse that had been at Heartland for four months. He needed a fun, lively home, and Amy felt sure that Melanie would be good to him.

"What do you think?" Ty said to her in a low voice.

"They're perfect for each other," Amy told him.

"I think so, too," Ty agreed, smiling at her.

After Melanie had dismounted and helped Amy untack Copper, the Satchwells scheduled a time the following week for Ty to come by and check out the stable where Melanie kept her horse.

"Bye, Copper," Melanie said, kissing the chestnut on the nose. "See you soon."

Amy watched the Satchwells leave and then headed up to Spartan's stall. She stroked his bay head. She was really pleased for Copper, but she still wasn't any closer to finding the right home for Spartan.

For the rest of the day, Lou seemed upset with Carl. She could not seem to forgive him for interfering with the Satchwells. However, when it came time for him to go back to Manhattan, Amy noticed that she had begun to relent.

"I'll miss you," Lou said as Carl put his bag in his car.

Carl put his arm around her shoulders. "Promise me you'll really think about Chicago this week?"

"Yes," Lou said, looking up at him. "I will."

They kissed and then Carl got into his car. "See you on Friday," he said as he started the engine. "Don't wear yourself out with all those dance preparations."

Amy watched Lou stand and wave until Carl's Saab disappeared down the drive.

She couldn't help feeling disappointed. After the way Lou had been so supportive that afternoon and positively angry with Carl over Copper, she had started to believe that Lou would turn down Carl's offer and stay at Heartland for good. However, looking at Lou's face, she didn't feel so sure anymore.

# Chapter Ten

The next day, Amy took Spartan out for another trail ride, taking care to stay on the paths where he would feel confident. Enjoying the sand and grass beneath his feet, he pulled at his reins and pranced excitedly. The trail ahead was long and grassy, so Amy leaned forward and let him canter. Spartan's long strides seemed to eat up the ground. Ahead of them a fallen tree lay half across the path. Amy tightened her hold on the reins. "Easy now, boy," she said, intending to slow him down in order to walk around the tree trunk. Spartan tossed his head and would not slow his pace.

Amy felt excitement surge through her. He wanted to jump it. She knew she should take things slowly with him, but the tree trunk looked so tempting. Although no one was there, she glanced around almost guiltily and then shortened her reins, angling him toward the low end of the trunk.

Spartan steadied his stride. Amy dug her knees into the saddle. They were three strides away, two, one, and then with a surge of power Spartan leaped into the air, clearing the log by a good three feet.

"Wow!" Amy gasped, patting his neck. Spartan snorted and, putting his head down, bucked with sheer delight. Amy laughed and pulled his head up, stopping him. His jump had so much spring!

She patted him for a moment knowing she should keep to the trail, but instead she trotted him back around the tree trunk. This time when she turned Spartan, she headed him for the highest part. As he plunged eagerly forward her heart leaped into her throat. What was she doing? But then she felt his smooth, powerful canter and her doubts disappeared. She sat down deep in the saddle. The tree trunk loomed in front of them, and suddenly they were over.

"Good boy!" Amy cried ecstatically. She patted his neck over and over again, feeling excitement buzz through her. Spartan was a natural jumper!

Amy didn't stay on the trail for long. She couldn't wait to tell Ty about Spartan's jumping.

"He was so good!" she told Ty, having found him the moment she got back. "He just flew over it both times!"

"You should try him in the training ring tomorrow," Ty said.

"I can't wait for you to see him!" Amy said, exhilarated by the thought.

The next day, after schooling Spartan on the flat, she hitched him to a post and put up a small jump. As she remounted she felt a shudder of nervousness. Maybe the day before had just been a fluke. But her worries melted when Spartan cleared the fence easily. Amy raised the jump just as Ty came to watch.

"Wow!" he said as Spartan cleared the jump by a couple of feet.

"He feels like he wants to go higher and higher," said Amy, her eyes shining. "I know he's overjumping a bit now, but he'll get over that with practice. He's incredible!"

From then on, every time that Amy rode Spartan she put up a jump. On Friday afternoon, she got Ty to help her set up an entire course of fences. "Here goes!" she called to him after she had warmed up Spartan.

Spartan threw his head up as she turned him into the first jump, but he soon settled into a perfect rhythm. He soared over jump after jump, evidently enjoying himself.

As they were approaching the last one, Amy suddenly realized that she had felt such sheer ability in only one other horse. And that was Pegasus. Excitement flooded through her. Spartan was smaller than Pegasus, but was there any reason why he couldn't one day be as good a jumper?

As they cleared the last jump, Ty clapped. "That was amazing!" he said.

"*He's* amazing!" Amy replied, her cheeks glowing. She looked around at the jumps. "I'd love to take him to a show — and do a long course of jumps. I bet he'd be fantastic!"

"Well, I guess he's not ready to compete yet, but there is a show at The Meadows on Sunday," Ty said. "You want to go? You could get him used to the atmosphere."

Amy stared at him. "Yes!" she said. "And they have a schooling ring there. You can pay to do warm-up courses. It would be a great experience for him!"

"Yeah," Ty said.

Amy's face suddenly fell. "But I bet Grandpa won't have time to drive me. It will be the day after the dance, and he'll be busy helping Lou with the cleanup."

"I'll take you if you want," Ty offered.

"Really?" Amy said. "But it's your day off."

Ty grinned. "I'd like to — it'll be fun. And if he jumps really well, we might find someone who would adopt him when he's ready."

Amy nodded, her thoughts reeling. She was going to take Spartan to a show! It seemed incredible that it was only a matter of days since he wouldn't even let her near him.

After Amy had put Spartan away in his stall, she went to the tack room to clean his tack. When she had finished, she went back to check on him. He was lying down in his stall, muzzle resting on the clean straw, legs curled underneath him. Amy smiled and quietly opened the door. Spartan looked at her but didn't get up.

"Taking a nap?" she murmured, kneeling down beside him in the straw and stroking his neck. Spartan snorted and rested his muzzle on her lap. Her fingers ran through his mane and he relaxed, his eyes half closed, his lower lip drooping slightly as he let her legs take the weight of his head.

Amy closed her eyes for a moment, letting her dreams play out in her head. She imagined Spartan clearing fence after fence at some big show, his scars not mattering, everyone cheering for him as he won class after class. He would be confident, happy. She let the most secret of her dreams come to the surface — Spartan living at Heartland, staying with her. She knew the horses that came to Heartland had to be rehomed, but Spartan was different. Mom had kept Pegasus after his accident because they had a special bond. Amy felt she was building that bond with Spartan, too. In her imagination, they galloped around an arena, a blue ribbon flying from

Spartan's bridle. Someday they might even become as good a team as Daddy and Pegasus had been.

She opened her eyes. "It could be," she whispered. "You and me, Spartan. I think we were meant to be together. I understand you better than anyone else ever could."

Spartan blew softly out through his nose.

"You'll be happy here," Amy said, kissing his head. "I'll *make* you happy." Feeling a great rush of affection, she put her arms around his neck and hugged him. As she did so she looked him in the eyes. His dark brown eyes were full of trust, but something was missing.

Amy's arms slackened their grip. People said that horses couldn't feel love, but she knew they were wrong. When she looked into Pegasus's or Sundance's eyes she could see love reflected there, welling deep and strong from the center of their being. But with Spartan, she couldn't sense the same connection. His eyes just held a sadness that hadn't gone away despite all her love for him.

He nuzzled her, but at that moment she realized that her dreams would always be just that — *dreams*. She could not bring the light back into his eyes. She couldn't make him love her. A lump formed in Amy's throat as she faced the bitter truth. Spartan was only hers for a little while — hers on loan, not hers to keep.

She stood up and walked slowly out of his stall.

"Amy! Amy!"

Amy looked up. There, jogging up the drive, her black curls bouncing, was Soraya!

"Soraya!" Amy gasped. She had been so busy thinking about Spartan that she had forgotten that Soraya came back from camp that day. Throwing away her worries, she raced down the yard to meet her friend. "You're home!"

"You noticed?" Soraya grinned. They hugged. As they pulled apart, Soraya looked around. "Gosh, it's good to be back." Her eyes sparkled. "Not that I didn't enjoy camp, of course."

Amy grinned. "It sounds like you enjoyed it a lot! So who's this Chris you keep going on about in your letters?"

"Chris?" Soraya questioned. "Amy, you're way behind! For the last two weeks it's been Kyle." She shook her head. "I can see we've got some serious catching up to do!"

❧

One hour and a bag of chocolate-pecan cookies later, Amy and Soraya were almost caught up with each other's news. Soraya had started going out with a boy named Kyle after a bonfire one night at camp, but they had decided not to keep dating when camp was over because they lived hours apart.

"He was really nice, though," Soraya said wistfully as she showed Amy his picture. "He said he's going to write."

Amy hugged her. "You'll meet someone around here." She looked at Soraya's disbelieving face. "I know you will!"

"All the halfway decent boys around here are taken, or they're madly in love with someone else," Soraya said. She shook her head at Amy. "Which reminds me — what's going on with you and Matt?"

Amy shook her head. "Oh, the same as usual. We're just good friends."

"You know he'll start going out with someone else soon," Soraya warned.

"Maybe you," Amy teased her.

"Yeah, right!" Soraya said. "I was thinking more like Ashley Grant — she's had her eye on Matt for ages."

"Well, she'll be at the dance tomorrow," Amy said, making a face. "I think she's just coming because she knows he'll be here. I bet she wears a debutante gown or something," Amy joked.

"It'll probably be totally expensive, too," Soraya said, shifting into a more comfortable position on Amy's bed. "So, how are all the preparations for the dance going? Is there a lot left to do?"

"Tons," Amy said. "We had a whole bunch of stuff delivered at lunchtime that needs organizing, and there's about a million napkins to be folded. Tomorrow is going to be just crazy!"

"I'll help with it all," Soraya offered. "I think it's a really cool idea — having the dance, I mean."

"Yeah, I do now," Amy admitted. "I didn't think so at first, but lots of people have been buying tickets. I guess Lou was right about it being a good way to raise money and get Mom's friends to come up here."

Soraya looked at her shrewdly. They had been friends since third grade and she knew all about Amy and Lou's stormy relationship. "How have you guys been getting along?"

Amy thought for a moment. "Better," she said. "We've been arguing on and off, but I think we're doing better."

"Your last letter said that Lou was thinking about moving to Chicago," Soraya said. "And by the way, can I remind you that we said we'd write at least three times a week? I only got one letter every ten days or so."

"I know — I'm sorry! It's just been crazy around here," Amy said. She shook her head. "Lou's still thinking about going to Chicago. I don't want her to, but she's just so into Carl that I think she might."

"And you still don't like him?"

Amy sighed. "I feel bad because I know he makes Lou happy, but there's just something about him. . . ." Amy heard a car outside and looked out the window. "Well that's the end of *that* discussion, here he is."

"Come on, I want to meet him," Soraya said, jumping up and heading for the door.

Amy followed her. "You don't. You really don't."

They went downstairs just as Carl came in. "I saw your mail had arrived," he said, handing a pile of letters to Jack. "So I thought I'd bring it in with me."

"Thanks, Carl," Grandpa said. "How was your trip?"

"Good, thanks," Carl replied. He nodded at Amy and Soraya. "Hi, kids."

"Hi," Soraya said politely, and then when Carl looked away she put a finger down her throat.

Amy rolled her eyes. *Kids! He's such a loser*, she thought.

Soraya smiled at her. "I'd better get back home. I promised Mom I wouldn't stay long. But I'll come over in the morning and help."

"OK," Amy said, walking to the door with her. "See you tomorrow. It's great to have you back!"

She watched Soraya disappear down the drive and then went into the kitchen. Carl had his arm around Lou.

"We've got so much to do!" Lou was saying to him. "I'm glad you're here."

"Don't worry. With you in charge it's bound to be a success," Carl said smoothly. "So how many people are coming?"

"Eighty-two at the last count," Lou said.

Carl looked casually at the mail. "And I guess a few more replies might have come today."

Lou picked up the pile to check. "Yes, it looks like it." Amy was about to go back upstairs when she heard Lou's voice change. "Hey, what's this?" Lou held up an envelope and frowned.

"Anything interesting?" Carl asked, looking over her shoulder.

"It's from Epstein and Webb," Lou said, holding an elegant cream envelope with an embossed crest in her hands. "Why are they writing to me?"

"Well, open it and see," said Carl.

Amy glanced at him. The slightest of smiles was playing at the corners of his lips.

Lou tore open the envelope and took out a letter. She read it, her eyes widening. Suddenly, she gasped. "They've offered me a job!" she cried, looking up. "An amazing one. And it's in Chicago." Lou flung her arms around Carl's neck. "It's actually in Chicago!"

"What? That's incredible!" Carl exclaimed. He hugged her. "It's fate, Lou. We were meant to be together in Chicago. Just think — we can get an apartment together, start a new life!"

"Oh, Carl!" Lou cried.

"That's great, Lou," Grandpa said quietly. Amy saw the sadness in his eyes.

Lou seemed to see it, too. She froze, the excitement fading quickly from her face. "Well, I'll have to decide if I should take it," she said hastily, stuffing the letter in her pocket and looking rather awkwardly from Grandpa to Amy.

"*If* you should take it?" Carl stared at her incredulously. "But Lou! This is the opportunity of a lifetime. You can't tell me you're thinking of turning it down?"

"It's a big move," Lou said defensively. "I'll have to call them and discuss the details."

"Lou!" Carl said in exasperation.

"Please, Carl," Lou said. "I need to think about it."

Carl stared at her for a moment, his face tightening. Suddenly, he picked up his bag. "I'm going to get changed," he said abruptly, striding out of the kitchen.

Lou sat down next to Jack at the table. "Oh, Grandpa," she sighed. As she looked up, Amy saw the confusion in her eyes. "What am I going to do?"

"What do you want to do?" Grandpa said, putting his arm gently on her shoulder.

"That's just it — I don't know."

"Don't take it, Lou. Stay here with us," Amy said softly, sitting down next to her.

"I *am* beginning to love it here. But I love Carl, too," Lou said. She shook her head. "And anyway, you don't really need me."

"Yes, we do!" Amy burst out.

"No, Amy. You don't," Lou said. "I make mistakes, like with the feed and trying to find homes for horses before they're ready. And you don't listen to my ideas, and that's hard for me. I'm used to being respected, I'm used to having my ideas really count."

"Lou, you can't know everything about Heartland right off the bat, but you've learned a lot. You just don't realize how much we need you," Amy said desperately.

Lou looked around distractedly. "Please, Grandpa," she groaned. "Tell me what to do."

"I can't do that, honey," he said, shaking his head. "You need to decide for yourself."

Lou sighed. "I know. But how?"

Grandpa leaned over and kissed her head. "Just follow your heart, Lou," he said softly. "Follow your heart."

# Chapter Eleven

"If I see one more red napkin I am going to go crazy!" Soraya declared as she folded a fork and knife into the last napkin and put it down on the table with a bang. "What else do we need to do?"

Amy looked up from unpacking a crate of glasses. "The tablecloths need to be laid out," she said. "But there's one more table to be put up first."

As she spoke, Matt came through the doorway carrying a table. "Where do you want this?" he asked.

"Over there," Amy said, pointing to a gap. "Thanks, Matt."

"What about the food?" Matt asked as he set the table upright.

"Well, Grandpa picked up the meat for the barbecue yesterday, and he and Lou are making lots of salads and desserts," Amy said. She had been put in charge of organizing the barn while Carl had been sent off to buy the drinks for the evening. She thought about the show the next day. She wasn't going to get a chance to give Spartan a bath. She'd just have to get up early in the morning despite the late night and give him a good brushing then.

"What next?" Matt said, coming over.

"If you unpack the plates," Amy said, pointing to the boxes of rented dishes, "I'll go and see if Carl has arrived with the drinks."

She went through to the kitchen. "Is Carl back?"

"Just," Lou said, looking up from slicing a tomato. "He's still outside."

Amy went out. Carl was leaning against the Heartland pickup with his back to her. Amy realized that he was talking on his cell phone, so she walked quietly toward the back of the truck to start unloading the drinks. She didn't want to disturb him.

She heard Carl laugh. "Of course, she doesn't know," he said. "She doesn't have any idea." Amy was trying not to listen, but his next words caught her off guard. "No, no. You've got it all wrong," he said. "Lou's not naive. She just trusts me." Amy froze at the mention of her sister's name. Carl shook his head. "The trouble with Lou is that she just doesn't know what will make her happy. All I've done is nudge her in the right direction, given fate a helping hand you could say."

Amy slowly started to back away. Her mind was reeling. She couldn't believe it! It sounded like Lou's job offer in Chicago was all a setup! Carl knew about it but was pretending he didn't. Amy suddenly remembered the way he had urged Lou to look at the mail the day before. She had to tell Lou what she had heard!

She tried to step backward toward the house, but then her foot caught on a stone and she tripped. Carl looked around. "Amy!" he said.

"Er — hi," Amy said. "I was just coming to help carry the drinks inside."

Carl's face visibly relaxed. "Oh, right." He spoke into his phone. "I'll talk to you later, Brett. Bye."

All the time Amy was helping Carl unload the drinks, she wished she could find Lou and tell her what she suspected. But after they had finished, she couldn't talk to her sister alone because Carl followed her into the kitchen.

Unfortunately, Lou was busy the rest of the day. Amy couldn't find a moment to talk to her without someone interrupting. In the end, she tried to push the bad news to the back of her mind, deciding it was best to tell Lou about it the next day, when things were quieter and her sister was less stressed.

By six o'clock, the barn was almost ready. The decorations were finished, the barbecue was lit, Grandpa had made his special punch, and the raffle tickets were stacked up and ready to be sold.

"Time to get changed!" Lou called, running through the kitchen. "It won't be long before people start arriving!"

Matt had gone home, but Soraya had brought her clothes over so that she could get changed with Amy.

"What do you think Ashley will be wearing?" she asked as she sat at Amy's mirror and brushed out her dark curls.

"Something revealing," Amy said. She looked over Soraya's shoulder and twisted her hair up. "What do you think, up or down?"

"Up!" Soraya said. She stood up and helped Amy knot her thick sun-streaked hair. "There!" she said, pulling down a few strands so that they framed Amy's face.

"Yeah. I like it," Amy said, pleased. She took out a pair of midnight blue cropped pants from her closet and pulled them on. Her mom had them bought them for her a year ago. She had hardly had a chance to wear them, but luckily they still fit, the slim cut making her look quite tall and elegant.

"Wow! Matt won't even recognize you in those!" Soraya giggled as Amy looked at herself in the mirror. Soraya pulled on a pair of black jeans and a strappy top made out of a silvery material. "What do you think?" she said, posing.

"You look marvelous!" Amy said dramatically. "Come on! Let's go!"

They hurried down the stairs and into the kitchen. Grandpa, Carl, and Ty were already there.

"You both look wonderful!" Grandpa said.

"Thank you," Soraya said.

Amy looked at Ty. He looked darkly handsome, his checked shirt emphasizing his broad shoulders.

"Wow!" he said, looking Amy up and down. "You look great!"

Amy raised her eyebrows teasingly. "You mean I don't normally?"

"Well, it's a change from your barn clothes," Ty commented. He grinned at her. "You really do look nice."

"Thanks." She smiled. "So do you." Their eyes met for a moment. Then Amy glanced away, feeling suddenly flustered.

Lou came into the kitchen from the barn. "I hope everyone shows up," she fretted.

Jack Bartlett opened the refrigerator and pulled out a jug of punch. "A toast!" he declared, getting out a tray of glasses. He filled the glasses and passed them around. "To the success of the dance!"

Amy looked at her sister. "To Lou!" she said impulsively.

"To Lou!" everyone echoed, clinking their glasses.

Lou smiled happily. "Thank you," she said.

"OK," Grandpa said. "We can't just stand around.

Someone needs to put out the appetizers and pour the drinks. Who's in charge of organizing the parking?"

Ty finished his glass and went outside to deal with the parking. Amy started opening bags of chips while Soraya went with Jack to the barn to help with the drinks.

Lou was just about to follow them when Carl caught her arm. "Here," he said, picking up their glasses and refilling them with punch. "Let's have another toast."

Amy glanced up.

"What to?" Lou asked.

Carl raised his glass. "To Chicago!"

Amy saw Lou falter, her glass stopping halfway to her mouth. "But, Carl, I haven't decided if I'm going yet."

Words leaped to Amy's lips, but she held them back.

"Come on, Lou," Carl exclaimed. "This is the perfect job, the perfect opportunity for us to be together. How can you still be undecided?"

"It's a hard decision to make," Lou said. "Surely you can see that. I need time to think about it."

"You don't have time!" Carl said, sounding irritated. "You have to schedule an interview by Tuesday."

"I know! I know!" Lou suddenly stopped. Amy saw her frown. "How do you know I need to have an interview by Tuesday?" she said to Carl. "I didn't tell you that."

For an instant, Carl looked horrified, but his expression

quickly smoothed. "Of course you did," he said quickly, putting a hand on her arm. "You must've forgotten."

"No, I didn't," Lou exclaimed. "I didn't want to tell you in case you started to pressure me. How did you know?" She suddenly took a step back, her eyes widening, her face going pale. *"You arranged it, didn't you?"* she whispered. "You *knew* about this job all along."

Carl looked for a moment as if he was going to deny it, but then he stepped forward. "Well, so what if I did?" he said. "Yes, OK, I arranged it, Lou. I want you to come with me — people *expect* you to come with me."

"You want me to come because of what our friends would think if I didn't?" Lou stared at him in horror.

"No — I —" Carl hastily changed his tone. "Lou, I only tried to get you a good job," he said, grabbing her hand. "Is that such a crime?"

"You tried to manipulate me! You deceived me!" Lou cried, snatching her hand away.

"Lou, listen —"

"No! You listen, Carl," Lou shouted. "I trusted you. How could you do this to me?"

Just then the back door opened and Scott and Matt walked in. Their greetings died on their lips as they took in the situation.

"Lou —" Carl moved forward.

Lou pushed him away. "Please don't," she pleaded. "I

can't go to Chicago with you. I'm going to need some time. Just go, and leave me alone."

"But —"

"Just go, Carl!" Lou said forcefully. "Go!" With that she ran out of the room, trying to stifle her tears.

Amy jumped to her feet, but before she could say anything Scott stepped forward. "You heard Lou," he said icily to Carl. "I think you'd better leave."

For a moment it looked as if Carl was about to hit him, but then he took a step back. "I'll get my things!" he snapped, and turning on his heel he stalked upstairs.

Scott looked out the window. "Amy, we've got to do something — the guests are arriving."

Amy looked at him in horror. "But what about Lou?"

"You should check on her," Scott said. "Matt and I will sort things out down here."

As Amy ran up the stairs, Carl came pushing past her, shoving things into his bag as he went.

"Bye to you, too," Amy muttered.

She hurried to Lou's bedroom. Her sister was lying facedown on the bed.

"Oh, Amy!" she sobbed, looking up. "What am I going to do?" She buried her head in her hands.

"You have to do what you think is right for you," Amy faltered. "Do you really want Carl to go to Chicago without you?"

Lou turned toward her sister. "All I know is, that after

all that's happened over the last few months, I definitely don't need anyone around whom I can't trust."

Amy knelt on the floor beside the bed and stroked Lou's hair. "Then I guess you're right," she said. "You're better off without him."

"How could he do that to me? I thought he respected me," Lou cried. "I thought he *loved* me."

Amy wrapped her arms around her sister. "Oh, Lou, we love you!" she said desperately. "Whatever you decide, Grandpa and I will always be here for you. No matter if you stay here or go back to New York, this will always be your home."

Lou started to sob even harder.

"And look, don't even worry about the dance," Amy consoled. "We can manage. Scott's greeting the guests. Everything is under control."

Lou sat up, tears running down her cheeks. "People are arriving already?"

Amy nodded. "But don't worry," she said quickly. "We can cope. You stay up here for as long as you want."

Lou brushed her tears away, "I organized it. I should be there."

"But Lou —"

"I'll be OK." With a sniff, Lou stood up and smoothed out her dress.

Amy felt her heart fill with admiration. *Lou is so strong,* she thought. She knew if their positions had been reversed she would have stayed in her room all night, crying her eyes out. But Lou was already looking into the mirror and fixing her makeup.

When she finally turned toward the door, the only hint of her inner turmoil was the tear-washed brightness of her eyes. "Come on," she said, taking a deep breath and reaching for Amy's hand. "Our friends are waiting."

&

Amy hurried around, filling up glasses and saying hi. She tried to keep an eye on Lou to make sure she was OK. But there was no need to worry. With a bright smile on her face she greeted people, telling them about the program for the evening and steering them toward the table where Ty was selling raffle tickets.

The Grant family arrived, Ashley looking stunning in a short green dress that had virtually no back.

*Very appropriate for a barn dance,* Amy thought sarcastically.

"Hello, Amy," Ashley said coolly.

"Hi," Amy replied, her voice curt.

Ashley looked around, her perfect eyebrows arching in surprise. "You've really got a lot of people here, haven't you?"

"That *was* the idea," Amy retorted, but Ashley wasn't listening. She had spotted Matt.

"Matt!" she called.

He looked around and came over. "Hi, Ashley," he said pleasantly.

"Hi," said Ashley, putting her hand on his arm. "I didn't know you were going to be here."

"Sure," Matt said in surprise. "I thought Scott had talked to your mom about it."

Ashley just raised her eyebrows and smiled coyly.

Shaking her head in amusement, Amy hurried away. Even Ashley's presence couldn't spoil the evening.

The barn filled up quickly. The noise level rose, glasses clinked, and as the band started up, people began moving onto the dance floor. Amy realized how right Lou had been all along. This was a terrific way to raise money! Everyone seemed to be having a wonderful time, and it was great to see all of Mom's friends. Amy thought about how proud Mom would have been of her oldest daughter.

She looked around for Lou and spotted her standing by the entrance to the barn with Grandpa and Scott. The earlier strain on her face had vanished completely. Scott said something and Lou laughed at him, her eyes sparkling. She looked genuinely happy and delighted as she watched all the guests having a good time.

Amy hurried over. "Lou! This is such a success — everyone's having a great time."

"They really are," Scott agreed. "Congratulations, Lou!"

"Thanks," Lou smiled. "And thanks for all your help."

"You're the one who pulled it together. I'm sorry I doubted you," Amy said decisively.

Lou looked slightly taken aback by her apology. "Thanks, Amy."

"And —" Amy struggled, finding the words difficult to say, "and — I think some of your other ideas for Heartland might work, too. You know, the brochure and things like that."

"Really?" Lou stared. "You'd really give them a chance?"

Amy nodded. "I've realized you know what you're doing when it comes to the business side of things." She looked at her sister, the words impulsively tumbling out of her. "Look, I was stupid not to listen to you before. Please say you'll stay, Lou. I promise I'll take your ideas seriously from now on. Don't go back to the city. Your home is here now and we *need* you."

Lou looked astonished and pleased. "Do you mean that?"

"Of course I do!" Amy exclaimed.

Lou looked at Grandpa, Scott, and Amy. "OK," she said, a smile suddenly spreading across her face. "I'll stay!"

# Chapter Twelve

In the early hours of the morning, the last guests finally left the party, and Amy dragged herself to bed. She glanced at her alarm clock as she turned off her light. Two o'clock! In only four hours she had to be up again to get Spartan groomed and ready for the show. "Oh, great," she groaned, turning over and falling asleep.

At six o'clock, Amy pulled herself out of bed and staggered out to the yard. First she had to feed the other horses and then tend to Spartan. However, she gradually managed to wake herself up by drinking several cups of coffee. By the time Ty arrived at eight-thirty, she was beginning to feel more cheerful. "You're going to be so good today," she told Spartan as she bandaged his tail to protect it in the trailer. "We'll show everyone just how special you are."

Spartan looked around at her and snorted almost as though he understood.

&

When they arrived at the show, Ty parked the trailer near the edge of the show ground, well away from the main commotion of the showrings and spectator stands. Spartan backed down the ramp and looked around excitedly, his ears pricked, his nostrils dilated.

"It's OK," Amy told him. "It's just a show ground. Do you remember, boy?"

Ty bent down to remove Spartan's leg wraps. "I'd take him for a walk around," he said, throwing them in a pile and then removing the tail bandage. "It will help him settle."

Amy nodded. She'd been thinking the same thing. "Come on, boy," she said, clicking her tongue. "Let's go."

Spartan pranced beside her, his neck arched. Amy thought he probably remembered going to shows with his previous owner. "And you might be going to shows again soon," she told him. "But not to compete in boring conformation classes, but in jumping classes so that everyone can see how good you are."

Just then, a rider cantered straight across their path

only a few feet in front of them. Spartan shied back in surprise. "Steady, boy!" Amy exclaimed.

Amy swung around.

There was Ashley Grant sitting astride a bay pony, looking smug, her clothes perfect and her pony gleaming. Despite the late night, Ashley looked as fresh as a daisy. "So, he's still nervous!" she said.

"Any horse would shy away if you did that to it!" Amy exclaimed.

"Temper, temper," Ashley mocked.

Amy shook her head in disgust and walked Spartan on. She ran her hand up and down his neck to keep him calm.

But there was no escaping Ashley. She rode right alongside Spartan. "So what have you brought *him* here for?" she said. "I heard he was vicious."

"Well, he's not," Amy said through gritted teeth. "He's healed."

Ashley laughed as she looked at Spartan's sides. "His scars certainly aren't!"

"So?" Amy demanded.

"So, you're not exactly going to get far with him in the showring, are you?" Ashley said.

"I'm not planning to take him in conformation," Amy retorted. "And you know that in jumping classes scars don't matter."

"Like a judge is *really* going to pick a horse with scars like that," Ashley said. She shook her head. "You're wasting your time and your money, Amy — and from what *I've* heard, Heartland hasn't got too much cash to spare just now." With a snide smile she cantered off.

"Just you wait till you see him jump, Ashley," Amy muttered. She suddenly felt a strong desire to enter Spartan in a class just so that she could wipe the smile off Ashley's perfect face. But entries had closed a week ago. "Next time," she promised Spartan as she watched Ashley enter the collecting ring on the bay pony.

Amy took Spartan back to the trailer. "I think I'll get on," she said to Ty. "He seems fine."

They tacked Spartan up. Amy pulled off the sweats she had been wearing to keep her tan breeches clean and pulled on her long boots and navy jacket. It felt good to be in show clothes again.

"Just take it easy," Ty said, holding the opposite stirrup as she mounted. "You don't want to overdo it."

Amy nodded. But as she patted Spartan she felt sure that he was up for it. He felt excited but not wild. She entered the schooling area where the other horses and riders were warming up. There were trainers shouting instructions, horses rushing past. Amy took a breath. If Spartan could cope with this, then he could cope with anything!

At first he was a little high-strung, but after ten minutes or so he lowered his head and started to listen to her signals. Once he was settled, Amy tried him over a jump. He didn't even hesitate. After they had warmed up over several small fences, Amy decided it was time to take him over a course in the schooling ring.

Ty saw her heading for the entrance and walked over to meet her. "He looks good. You think he's ready?"

Amy nodded, excitement gathering in the pit of her stomach. This was the moment she had been waiting for.

At the gate to the training ring Ty paid an official the schooling fee. "Are the jumps OK at this height?" the official asked. Ty turned to Amy.

Amy looked around the elaborate course. The jumps were about three feet six, higher than she would have ideally liked. "They're fine," she said. When she was riding Spartan she felt as if she could jump anything!

"Good luck!" Ty called as she rode into the ring.

Shortening her reins, Amy patted Spartan's neck. "This is it, boy," she said, her excitement growing as she noticed a few spectators watching casually at the fence. "Let's show everyone what you can do."

Spartan's ears flickered. She gave him a squeeze with her legs, and he moved forward into a smooth canter. Amy circled once and then turned to the first jump — an imposing post and rails. Spartan's stride was even and perfect. He cleared the fence easily, his ears pricked forward as he headed to the second fence in the outside line.

Amy stayed with his steady rhythm as they cleared fence after fence. She could hardly believe what a great understanding they had. She cantered him toward the final jump — a tricky parallel spread — right next to the edge of the ring.

"Gerry?" she heard a girl's voice gasp from the ringside.

Amy felt Spartan's step falter. They were only three strides away from the fence and they had too much momentum to pull away. Amy closed her legs around his sides and pushed him on. "Come on, boy," Amy whispered.

Spartan responded. With an enormous surge of power he gathered himself and took off over the wide fence. It seemed like a minute had passed before they landed safely on the other side.

There was a smattering of applause from those watching.

"Good boy!" Amy cried, forgetting about the voice from the crowd in her sheer delight. Patting him constantly she trotted over to the gate. "Wasn't he great?" she cried to Ty.

"The best!" Ty called back.

"What a nice round," the official said to Amy. "You've got a horse with a lot of potential. You're sure to come away with lots of ribbons."

Amy just smiled as she slid off Spartan's back and flung her arms around his neck. "You were wonderful!" she said. Then, taking Spartan's reins she led him away with Ty.

"Um . . . excuse me," a voice said tentatively behind them.

Amy looked around. A girl about her own age with wavy dark hair was standing there. She was dressed in show clothes and her cheeks looked slightly flushed. "Is that Gerry . . . Geronimo?"

"Yes," Amy said in confusion, turning Spartan around. "At least he *was*. Who are you?"

Before the girl had a chance to reply, Spartan nickered and pulled Amy forward with a toss of his head.

"Oh, Gerry," the girl breathed in delight. "I thought I was never going to see you again."

Amy felt an ache of envy as Spartan nuzzled the girl's hands. Who was she? "Umm . . . sorry, but I don't know who you are," Amy said rather shortly.

The girl looked up at her, her brown eyes suddenly flustered. "Oh, I'm Hannah Boswell. Larry Boswell's my grandfather. I've known Gerry since he was born. I recognized him as soon as I saw you in the ring."

Amy's eyes widened in astonishment. "You're Mr. Boswell's granddaughter?"

Hannah nodded. "I live on the farm with him and Grandma. Are you Amy?" When Amy nodded, Hannah smiled. "Grandpa told me about you. About your rescue center and how you've been looking after Gerry."

"What are you doing here?" Amy said, still trying to get over the fact that she had met Larry Boswell's granddaughter.

"I'm here for the show," Hannah said. "I was supposed to be riding in an equitation class."

Ty frowned. "I thought I'd seen you before," he said. "Do you have a dapple-gray pony?"

"That's right," Hannah said. "We don't usually travel this far for a show, only when there's a big class like today."

"You're really good," Ty said. "I saw you at Middlebrook."

Amy felt a flash of jealousy as Hannah smiled at Ty.

"Thanks," the other girl said. "I'm just lucky I've got Sinbad." Her eyes glowed. "He'd make any rider look wonderful."

Amy's jealousy disappeared as she heard Hannah Boswell praising her pony, and she felt herself starting to like her. "What did you mean you were *supposed* to be in an equitation class?" she asked curiously.

"Sinbad's gone lame," Hannah said. "He must have knocked himself on the ride over. It's not too bad, but I'm not going to risk riding him. I'm just going to cancel my entry. It's typical though that it happened today when there's a big qualifying class." Although she smiled, Amy saw that her eyes looked sad. Hannah looked around. "I have to tell my Grandma that you're here. I know she'll want to say hello. Is that OK?" she asked.

"Yeah, sure," Amy said.

"I'll be back in a minute," Hannah promised, setting off across the show ground.

"She seems nice," Amy said, turning to Ty. Amy didn't compete in equitation herself; she preferred the hunter division where the emphasis was on the horse and not the rider. Still, she knew Hannah must be disappointed.

Ty nodded. "She's a really good rider," he said. "Whatever she says, her pony doesn't look that easy. I think she has real talent."

Amy patted Spartan thoughtfully.

Hannah came running back. "Grandma's coming!" she panted, her dark hair tousled. Spartan pulled toward her and nuzzled her.

"Umm . . ." Amy took a deep breath, the idea spilling out of her. "Hannah — would you like to ride Spartan — I mean *Gerry* — for your equitation class?"

She saw Ty turn and stare at her. Hannah's eyes widened. "Ride Gerry? But you don't even know if I can ride!" Hannah said.

"Well, Ty's seen you, and he says you're good," Amy said. She glanced at Ty. "That's enough for me."

"Well, I'd love to ride him!" Hannah said. She scanned Amy's face anxiously. "You really wouldn't mind?"

"No," Amy said slowly, watching as Spartan breathed on Hannah's hand. "No, I wouldn't mind."

Hannah smiled and then suddenly waved at someone over Amy's shoulder. "Grandma! I'm here!"

Mrs. Boswell had short gray hair and was dressed in jeans. Her face lit up as she saw Spartan. "Gerry!" she said.

Spartan nickered softly. Mrs. Boswell smiled and rubbed his head. "Well, hi, boy. It's sure good to see you looking so well." She turned to Amy and Ty, holding out her hand and smiling. "Hello, I'm Shelley Boswell."

They shook hands and introduced themselves. Hannah quickly told her grandma about taking Spartan in the equitation class. "I'd better get my hat and saddle," she said. "My class is next."

"I'll ride Spartan around," Amy said. "To get him warmed up for you."

"And I'll grab a brush and towel so we can go over him before you enter the ring," Ty said.

Amy rode Spartan into the schooling area. They trotted around, his strides long and smooth, his ears flickering as he followed Amy's signals. She asked him to canter and rode him in two neat figure eights. "Good boy," she whispered, stroking his neck.

Seeing Hannah outside the ring with her saddle, Amy brought Spartan back to a walk and rode over to where Hannah stood.

"Is it okay if I use my saddle?" Hannah asked.

Amy nodded and dismounted. Taking a deep breath, she ran up the stirrups, undid the girth, and then slid her saddle from Spartan's back.

"Are you still sure this is OK?" Hannah asked, looking at her.

Amy swallowed. "I'm sure."

Amy held tight on to Spartan's reins as Hannah lifted her own saddle onto Spartan's back. Spartan nuzzled her hands as Hannah tightened the girth. Amy quickly kissed his nose.

"I really appreciate it," Hannah said, standing back. "It's my last chance to qualify for the state finals."

Feeling her heart twist, Amy held out Spartan's reins.

As Hannah took the reins, their eyes met.

"Good luck," Amy whispered, still holding on.

"Thank you," Hannah said softly.

Slowly, Amy let go.

🙡

After Hannah had ridden around for a bit, and had taken Spartan over a few jumps, she came over to Ty and Amy. Ty gave Spartan a quick brush over. "You look good on him," he said.

Amy nodded. She had been watching carefully as Hannah rode around. It was obvious that Ty was right. Hannah was a very talented rider — her hands were light and her seat was perfectly balanced. Spartan looked relaxed and happy.

"I always loved riding him when he was at Grandpa's, but I had never jumped him," Hannah said. She smiled. "He feels strange after Sinbad."

"How many hands is Sinbad?" Amy asked.

"Fourteen two. He's getting a bit too small for me now. Grandpa said he'll buy me a new horse. But I just can't find one I really like." She smiled. "I'll keep Sinbad, too, of course. I'd never sell him."

Shelley Boswell came over. "Hannah! You need to report to the announcer so they know you're here."

Hannah grinned nervously. "Well, here goes. Wish me luck!"

"Oh, Hannah?" Amy said. Hannah looked back. "If he seems to hesitate before a fence, give him a tiny nudge and he'll be fine. He just needs a little reassurance sometimes."

Hannah nodded. "Thanks," she said.

Ty and Amy went to watch at ringside. "Look, it's Ashley!" Amy said, elbowing Ty as Ashley trotted into the ring. She was on a different horse — a beautiful gray with a thick tail that floated behind it like a waterfall. Ashley asked the horse to canter and headed smoothly toward the first jump.

Amy watched carefully. When she competed with Sundance against Ashley, it was usually in the pony hunter classes where it was the pony that was judged and not the rider. But equitation was different. It was the rider's style and ability that mattered and Amy had to admit it — Ashley was good. She had perfect posture and her smile never left her face. "She doesn't seem to do anything wrong!" Amy said aloud.

"I don't know," Ty said critically. "She's a bit stiff in the shoulders."

At the next jump Ashley's horse took off too late, but Ashley recovered well.

"She'll lose points there," Ty commented.

"Not many," Amy said.

"But you can tell she doesn't have a real connection with the horse," Ty said. "I mean, her riding is technically precise, but there's no bond there. Some judges care about those things, too."

Ashley finished the course with a circle and rode out.

"Is Hannah next?" Amy asked.

But there was one competitor before her — a boy on a large chestnut pony.

Shelley Boswell came to join them. "It was really kind of you to let Hannah ride Gerry," she said to Amy.

"No problem," Amy said.

"Larry told me what happened on his visit to you. You must think he's not very devoted to his horses," Shelley Boswell said.

Amy wasn't sure what to say. "Well . . . um . . ."

"It's all right, honey," Shelley Boswell said, smiling. "I can imagine what he must have been like. But Larry's not a cruel man, despite what you might think. All his life he's had to work hard. He built his business from scratch, and he's always had the rule that each of his horses has to pay its way. That's what's made him successful. But I think it broke his heart to let Gerry go, and he sure does miss him. We all do."

"Hannah's up!" Ty said as the chestnut pony left the ring and Hannah trotted in.

Spartan's ears were pricked. He threw his head up for a moment when he saw the fences but then listened to Hannah's signals and lowered his head. They moved smoothly into a canter and then turned toward the first jump.

Amy held her breath. But Spartan sailed over it easily with a foot to spare.

"He jumps big, doesn't he?" Shelley Boswell said.

Amy nodded. She was full of admiration for Hannah's riding. It wasn't easy to stay in the perfect position on a horse that jumped as high as Spartan, but Hannah managed it. Her back was straight, her head up, and her heels down. "Hannah looks really good on him," she said.

Shelley Boswell nodded. "Hannah loves jumping — always has. She's going to look for a horse to compete in the jumper division next."

Amy nodded, concentrating on the ring. Hannah and Spartan were halfway around the course now.

As they cantered around the far side of the ring they made a perfect picture. There appeared to be a bond between them, a special connection. Amy suddenly felt her eyes blur with tears. She glanced at Ty. She was glad that she had listened to him and decided to let Hannah ride Spartan. She could see from his face that he felt the same.

"They look great together," he said softly.

Amy nodded. She couldn't help but think that Spartan really looked happy jumping with Hannah.

Ty touched her hand. "Thanks for trusting me — about Hannah's riding, I mean."

"I always trust you," Amy said, surprised by the words that sprang to her lips.

"Just one more fence to go!" she heard Shelley Boswell say.

With a start, Amy turned her eyes back to the ring. With perfect timing, Spartan cleared the last jump, and the audience burst into applause. Hannah circled him past the entrance and then, patting him as if she were never going to stop, brought him back to a walk.

Amy, Ty, and Shelley Boswell hurried over to meet her. "That was incredible!" Amy said.

"Great job!" Ty said, smiling at Hannah.

"He was perfect!" she said, jumping off. "Amy, thanks for the advice — I gave him a little nudge when he seemed nervous and he was fine." Hannah turned to Spartan and rubbed his face. "You were fabulous!"

Amy smiled. At that moment everything seemed really good. And then Amy saw Ashley and Val Grant walk past them, their faces set. They had obviously seen Hannah's round. "I guess Ashley won't be so quick to put Spartan down anymore," Amy said with a grin. She stroked the horse's nose, and he pushed against her hand.

It was a nerve-racking wait for the results, but at last the loudspeaker crackled into action. "Results of equitation over fences, 14- to 17-year-olds," it said.

Hannah looked nervously at Amy. "You know, I don't even care if I place. It's enough to have had such a great round."

Amy looked at Hannah as the announcer continued.

"In first place, number three-six-five — Hannah Boswell on Geronimo."

"You did it, Hannah!" Amy cried. "You qualified for state finals."

"Oh, my gosh!" Hannah gasped in astonishment. She hugged her grandmother and then turned to Spartan. "Gerry, we won!" Suddenly, Hannah was mounting Spartan. Mrs. Boswell brushed over her riding boots, and Amy hurried to check Spartan's girth.

"Go on. You're in!" Ty said, seeing the ringmaster waiting.

Grinning from ear to ear, Hannah rode into the ring.

It didn't take long for the ribbons to be given out. Ashley was in second place, and she looked thunderous, not even nodding a thank-you as she received her red ribbon.

As Hannah turned to lead Spartan out of the ring, Amy felt Ty's hand on her shoulder.

"You know, that was a really nice thing to do," he said softly.

Amy looked into his eyes. "Thanks," she replied.

🐎

"Thank you so much for letting me ride Gerry. I mean Spartan," Hannah said a little while later as she and Amy took Spartan back to the Heartland trailer. "He really is wonderful — you are going to take him to lots more shows, aren't you?"

Amy's heart sank slightly. "Well, it depends when we find him a new home."

"But why don't you keep him?" Hannah said, sounding surprised.

Amy shook her head. "At Heartland it's our policy to try to rehome the horses that we care for."

Hannah looked sadly at the horse. "Poor Gerry. He seems so happy with you."

"Probably not as happy as he could be." Amy sighed. She decided to confide in Hannah. "I feel as if there's this bit of his heart that's locked away," she said. "The only time I've seen him look truly happy was when your grandfather came and just now, with you."

"I do think Gerry was happy with us before he was stolen. If only Grandpa would take him back or if I could have him." Hannah looked upset. "It's not fair," she said.

Amy stared at her, an idea leaping into her mind. "Well, why can't you? You said you were looking for a horse. You want one that can jump. Spartan would be perfect!"

Hannah looked startled. "Me have *Gerry* — but Grandpa would never agree. He gets upset whenever Gerry's name is mentioned."

Amy's flicker of hope died. "Oh." She sighed.

"But maybe it could work!" Hannah said, her face looking as if she was figuring out a difficult problem. "I can't tell Grandpa that I want Gerry because he'll say no. But if I call him and say that I've found an amazing jumper that I want to buy . . . and if I just show up with him —"

Amy stared at her. "But what would your grandpa say? Wouldn't he go crazy?"

Hannah shook her head. "I don't think so. Despite

what he says, he really misses Gerry, and I'm sure he would never be able to turn him away." She grabbed Amy's arm, her eyes suddenly shining with excitement. "Amy! This could work. This could really work! Let me ask Grandma and see what she says."

〰

It took Hannah only a few minutes to persuade her grandmother that her plan could work. Amy called Lou on her cell phone to tell her the news.

"So he's going now?" Lou said in astonishment.

"Yes," Amy said. "The Boswells' trailer isn't big enough, but Ty said that he'll drive Spartan and me there in our trailer."

"But it's Ty's day off!" Lou said. "Look, ask him to bring the trailer back here, and I'll drive you and Spartan to the Boswells'."

"OK," Amy said. She switched off the phone and went to tell Ty.

Soon it was all arranged. Hannah and Shelley Boswell would go ahead with Sinbad and let Larry Boswell know about the "new" arrival.

"I'll get his old stall ready for him," Hannah said, giving Spartan a last pat before heading off with her grandma. "Now, you've got the directions?"

Amy nodded.

Hannah grinned at her. "Then we'll see you in a couple of hours."

❧

Ty drove Amy and Spartan back to Heartland. "Well, I guess this is good-bye, fella," he said, going into the trailer as Lou got her things together. He patted Spartan. "Be happy."

"He will," Amy said softly, looking at Spartan's handsome bay head.

Lou came out of the house. "Are we ready?"

Amy nodded. "See you tomorrow, Ty. Thanks for everything."

"No problem," Ty said smiling. He turned and walked off down the yard. Amy quickly got into the pickup.

Lou opened the door and jumped in beside her. "Okay, let's go!"

As the trailer bumped down the drive, Amy heard Spartan whinny. A sharp memory of a time, three months ago, when Spartan had been in the back of the trailer and Mom, not Lou, had been sitting beside her, leaped into her mind. Then, Amy and her mom had been trying to save Spartan. She glanced at her sister — now she and Lou were giving him a chance to be happy.

She swallowed as she thought about the last three months. She had lost so much, but looking at Lou now and remembering her decision to stay at Heartland, she suddenly realized she had gained something, too.

❧

Larry Boswell's stud farm was set deep in the rolling countryside south of Heartland. Amy watched as they drove past farm after farm. At last they reached Dancing Grass Stables. Dark wooden fences separated the paddocks from the road. A heavy wooden sign swung in the slight breeze.

"Looks like we're here," said Lou.

Amy felt a prickle of apprehension as they turned up the drive. What if Hannah was wrong? What if Larry wouldn't accept Spartan and they had to take him back again?

Lou drove up to the front of the farmhouse, and they got out and looked around. No one came out. "I'll go and knock," Lou said. But there was no reply at the front door, so Lou went around to the back.

Amy went to check on Spartan. Seeing her, he gave a little nicker. Amy stepped slowly through the side door of the trailer. Spartan's dark eyes looked at her calmly. She wondered what the future would hold for him. What would Mr. Boswell decide?

Just then she heard the sound of voices approaching from the back of the trailer. "That's the Heartland trailer!" she heard Larry say. His tone turned harsh. "What are *they* doing here?"

Amy froze and then she heard Hannah speak. "They're delivering the horse I rode at the show, Grandpa. The one I told you about."

Suddenly, she heard Lou's voice. "Hi," her sister said, coming from the direction of the house. "We finally got here. Hello, Mr. Boswell."

"Hi." Amy heard Larry say gruffly.

"So, are you ready to see him, Grandpa?" Hannah asked eagerly.

"Amy's in there with him," Lou said.

Hannah suddenly appeared at the side door. "Amy, hi! Are you ready to bring him out?" She must have seen the concern on Amy's face because she gave a reassuring smile. "Don't worry," she said in a low voice. "It'll be fine. Trust me."

She disappeared, and Amy heard the locks on the ramp being undone. She placed a hand on Spartan's bay neck and felt the warmth of his satin-smooth coat. *Is this finally good-bye?* she thought. After everything that had happened to them both, it seemed almost impossible to believe.

"Spartan, you're back at Dancing Grass Stables," Amy said. "We've been through so much since the last time you were here." She put her cheek against his graceful head. "I'm going to miss you, boy, but I think this is where you belong."

Amy heard the ramp being lowered and she steadily led Spartan out.

Larry Boswell stared at Spartan incredulously, but before he could speak, Spartan nickered and pulled at the lead rope. Amy let go of the halter and stood back. The horse walked briskly over to his owner. Lifting his muzzle to Larry's face, he snorted and then buried his head in Larry's shoulder.

"Gerry!" Larry Boswell said, reaching out and touching the horse's neck. Spartan pushed against Larry's chest and nuzzled him, his nostrils flaring as he breathed in his owner's scent. "Oh, Gerry," Larry murmured.

"Grandpa, Gerry's the horse that I won on at the show," Hannah said softly. "You wouldn't have believed it. He was amazing. He's the horse I want." She went up to her grandpa and took his hand. "Please say that I can keep him. Please say you'll let Gerry stay."

Amy held her breath as Larry hesitated. Then, she noticed a tear running down his cheek. "Yes," he said, brushing it quickly away and looking at Hannah. "Of course he can stay."

❧

Soon Spartan was settled happily back in his old stall as if the immense trauma of the past few months had never happened.

"We should be going," Lou said to Shelley Boswell. "I'm glad it all worked out so well in the end."

"Me, too, honey." Shelley Boswell smiled.

Amy said good-bye to Hannah and then looked over to where Spartan was gazing out of his stall. He turned his head toward her, his ears pricked, his silky forelock tumbling down over his handsome face. The happiness in his eyes was unmistakable. Amy felt a lump of tears gather in her throat. At last, Spartan's heart was at home.

Amy bit her lip and thought of all she had promised Spartan, and how relieved she was to know he was now happy. She smiled through her tears and blew Spartan a kiss. She took one last look at him and turned away.

Swallowing painfully, she walked over to the pickup where Lou was waiting.

"I'll write!" Hannah called. "And send you photos."

As Amy opened the door and got in, she saw Larry Boswell walking over to Spartan's stall. Spartan whinnied softly, and Amy saw Larry's face crease into a delighted smile.

Suddenly, she felt Lou squeeze her hand. "You did the right thing, Amy," she said. "Everyone needs a home, and you know that Heartland would never have been Spartan's."

Amy looked at her sister. "But it is yours now, isn't it, Lou?" she asked, her words full of hope.

Lou smiled. "Yes," she replied. "It is." Her eyes met Amy's as she started the engine. "Come on," she said softly. "Let's go home."